Liffey Rivers And The Secret Of The Mountain Of The Moon

Visit www.booksurge.com to order additional copies.

BRENNA BRIGGS

LIFFEY RIVERS AND THE SECRET OF THE MOUNTAIN OF THE MOON

2008

Liffey Rivers And The Secret Of The Mountain Of The Moon

AUTHOR'S NOTE

Following the last chapter, in **Liffey's Lingo**, you will find a detailed explanation, along with a pronunciation guide, for the Irish words used in this book.

For Virginia Rose Morrow
***

CHAPTER ONE

Thick clouds smothered the top of the mountain where Liffey Rivers sat on a large rock near Queen Maeve's grave. It felt like she was sitting in a bowl of mashed potatoes. She could no longer see her father. She could only hear him breathing in and out from somewhere in the fog.

Liffey wanted this crazy day to be *over*. She felt light headed, like a bubble floating around waiting to pop.

First, there had been the feis at Beltra, where she had met Sinead and actually enjoyed herself. She may have made her first *real* friend today.

Then there was the frightening encounter with the art thieves and the endless *questions* people expected her to answer. As if. As if *she* knew anything more than anybody else did! Teams of agents and investigators, who probably knew more now about Liffey Rivers than she knew about herself, had descended upon little Beltra Hall in County Sligo.

To top it all off, her father *had* to make her watch that videotape! If she had just kept her big mouth *shut* about how the lady she saw in that tape could *not* be her dead mother, her father would probably be making up mountain 'Knock, knock!' jokes right now while they were waiting for the clouds to clear. Instead, there was an awkward silence between them which had never been there before.

Liffey could not think of *anything* to say to her father. She would probably have to risk asking him a history question, if they were ever going to even speak to each other again. Something he would know very little, or better yet, *nothing* about. Then he would not be able to start one of his endless, boring lectures which she would immediately regret since she was basically *trapped* on top of this mountain with him.

Liffey was sure Robert Rivers had not believed her when she told him that the 'dead' woman in his ten-year-old videotape could not be her mother.

"If my mother is dead, then she was *not* the woman in that tape because I was *definitely* with the lady in that tape two years ago when I was eleven," Liffey had informed her father, who looked like he was going to have a stroke. Her father reminded her that her mother had been in a plane that *exploded* ten years ago. Liffey remained unconvinced, but kept her mouth zippered so her father would not explode too.

Liffey had spent several hours with the tape lady during a layover at the airport in Houston. The three-hour wait had passed by quickly while they devoured Tex-Mex chili and talked about the Seattle Space Needle.

Liffey had immediately liked this lady. Unlike most adults, when she asked Liffey questions, she really *listened* to Liffey's answers. She also knew a lot about Irish dance, and she was beautiful. Liffey had been dazzled by the diamond 'M' she wore on a chain around her neck, like Queen Anne Boleyn wore a silver 'B' in her royal portrait hanging in London.

When Liffey had asked her what the 'M' stood for, the lady replied that 'M' was the beginning letter of both her first and last names. Just then, a loud boarding announcement blasted over the intercom and Liffey did not hear what those names were. Liffey meant to ask her again on the plane, but then forgot all about it because it seemed like she already *knew* this lady. Liffey felt comfortable and natural with her.

It was almost like...

Liffey did not realize she never *had* learned the diamond 'M' lady's first and last names until right now, right here, sitting on top of Knocknarea. "*Why* didn't I ask her again?" she thought bitterly, squinting through the fog at the dim outline of her father.

***

"What does 'Knocknarea' mean, daddy?" Liffey inquired half-heartedly, trying to forget about the 'M' lady for a minute and get her father talking again. She was fairly certain that this question was a safe one, because her father did not speak Irish. Therefore, he could not *possibly* go into a lengthy, university-level kind of explanation. Liffey was very alarmed then, when Robert Rivers began to answer her question with some authority.

"'Knock' means hill, or mountain, Liffey. And 'rea' probably means moon, although it could mean 'king,' or just a 'flat place.' But many scholars think that Knocknarea means 'mountain of the moon.' I'm afraid that's about all I can tell you."

"Why can't *all* his lectures be four sentences long?" thought Liffey, very relieved that they were talking again. This conversation was even kind of interesting because Liffey had always been captivated by the moon.

And the secrets it kept on its dark side.

CHAPTER TWO

The clouds started to break up and Liffey could finally see her miserable father. He looked so sad, Liffey almost wished the clouds would come back to hide them from each other again and make things less painful. Liffey searched her tired brain for something else to talk about. Food might work. "I'm *hungry*, daddy. Let's get down this mountain and find some *chili!*"

"*Chili?*" said Robert Rivers in a trembling voice, rising from his rock like Dracula from his coffin. "Why *chili*, Liffey?"

"Here we go again," Liffey muttered. "Daddy is so bizarre lately. I am going to have to figure out what to do about him first thing when we get home."

"Why *not* chili, daddy?" Liffey replied good-naturedly, hopping up from her perch and very much hoping Robert Rivers was not going to start acting like a madman again.

"*What* made you think of chili, Liffey?"

Why was he cross-examining her? Am I on a witness stand? Is wanting chili some kind of *crime*? Am I on *trial* for wanting to eat a bowl of chili? Liffey was exasperated. Was her father going to get all schizo now about chili, like he had about the taxis?

"Well, I don't know, daddy," Liffey answered as patiently as she could manage. "I *guess* I *like* chili and I was thinking about the lady in the tape and how she *loved* the chili at the Houston airport and it made me hungry for it."

Robert Rivers stared straight ahead and looked like he was going to have a complete meltdown. Like someone in a movie with their eyes bulging out who had just been shot through the heart with an arrow sticking out. Was he going to start gasping for air next and keel over? Just as Liffey was trying to figure out if this might be a medical emergency, he turned away from her and spoke in a strangled whisper, "Chili was your mother's *favorite* food, Liffey. She would go *anywhere* for good chili. She had 50 chili recipe books."

***

Picking their way down the side of Knocknarea should have been relatively easy, but banks of fog kept closing in, interrupting their progress.

"Let's play 'Simon Says,'" Liffey suggested playfully, trying to ease the tension which was steadily mounting again between father and daughter. Robert Rivers, who was shuffling slowly downward just inches ahead, did not reply.

"*You* know, daddy. *You* say, 'Simon says take ten baby steps.' Then I move ten baby steps. Then you try to *trick* me and say, 'Take ten baby steps' without saying that 'Simon *says*' to take the steps. If I *do* take the steps, then I'm out."

"Out of what, Liffey?"

"Out of 'Simon Says,' daddy. Then it's my turn to be Simon and try to trick you."

"Liffey, in case you haven't noticed, we are having some trouble here. I can barely even see the ground we are walking on, let alone tell you what kind of 'Simon Says' steps to take."

"All right then," Liffey said, continuing her efforts to release her father from his frozen brain condition. "Knock, knock!"

"Who's there?" Robert Rivers answered automatically.

"Shelby."

"Shelby who?"

"Shelby comin' 'round the mountain when she comes..."

Liffey was greatly relieved when her father groaned and laughed a little. This 'Knock, knock!' joke seemed to cheer Robert Rivers up quite a bit. But when she said, "Your turn, daddy," he mechanically replied, "Liffey, I am too mentally drained to think up a good mountain 'Knock, knock!' joke at the moment."

Liffey sighed and continued to carefully pick her way down the steep incline. She could not risk spraining her ankle and ruining her autumn feiseanna schedule. She was determined to place first in her Novice Hornpipe at the Fall Festival Feis in two weeks, and her ankles had to hold up.

It had taken them almost an hour to get up the mountain and from the way things were going, it was going to take them considerably longer to get back down. She guessed that it was long past dinner time now, because she could hear her stomach growling through the swirling mist like some kind of monster trudging along next to her.

***

By the time they passed through the sheep gate near the bottom of the mountain, it was almost dark. Liffey estimated it had taken them over three hours to inch their way back down Knocknarea into the deserted car park. She was not about to bring the chili subject up again, but she was very, *very* hungry. Usually after a feis, she would eat shrimp fried rice. She tried to think of a safe food subject now. Liffey had not known until today that her mother had loved chili. "What kind of menu should I suggest for dinner tonight?" She did not want her father to start foaming at the mouth again. "Maybe

I had better not eat at all and just go hungry," Liffey decided. "It's way too risky talking about food."

***

Before she collapsed into the car and tried to pretend things were normal, she looked back at the mountain and saw that an immense, rust-colored moon was rising. 'Blood Moon' Liffey thought excitedly. She remembered her father telling her that was what the ancient Celts called their September moon. It was the time when domestic animals were butchered and prepared for the long, bleak Irish winters.

She leaned back against the car door, admiring the rusty moon and plotting her next move with her despondent father. They were *supposed* to have climbed the mountain and then gone looking for caves. Instead, Liffey had been tricked into a video flashback that made no sense to her whatsoever. "If the lady in that tape really *is* my mother, then she could *not* be dead, because I *definitely* ate chili with that lady in Texas two years ago," Liffey thought for the hundredth time.

Ghosts do not eat chili!

Liffey tapped lightly on the passenger window to get her father's attention. The door was locked. When she turned to say goodbye to the mysterious rising moon, her mouth dropped open. The moon was sailing through the inky clouds like a giant frisbee. Then it lurched to a halt right above Queen Maeve's cairn and slivers of white moonlight began streaming down from it like a waterfall. Was there going to be some kind of extra-terrestrial *invasion*?

Liffey held her breath, trying hard not to blink, keeping her gaze fixed on the apparition. When the black clouds eventually erased the waterfall moon, Liffey was left awestruck with the impression she had just witnessed a supernatural event. She had an almost over powering impulse to run back up Knocknarea, even though it was getting dark. She had to force herself to turn away from the mountain and focus back on her father.

Liffey wanted to cry. Robert Rivers was sitting in the rented Picasso brooding, staring blankly at the steering wheel. He had not seen anything. He had not even unlocked her door.

***

Liffey considered telling her crestfallen father what he had just missed.

Maybe she should also tell him that the diamond 'M' lady knew how to Irish dance?

When Liffey was practicing her hornpipe steps in the Houston airport terminal, the 'M' lady had offered some really good advice about how Liffey could improve her foot extension. Liffey had asked her if she were an Irish dancer and her reply was, "I'm not sure. I don't think so."

What kind of answer was *that?* "I don't *think* so." Wouldn't somebody *know* whether or not they were an Irish dancer? Since Liffey had only been eleven at the time, and was a very polite young lady, she had not questioned the diamond 'M' lady further.

Liffey thought it would be better *not* to share this particular memory about the diamond 'M' lady with her father right now, because she instinctively knew Robert Rivers would not be able to process it without flipping out again. She knew very well that her mother had been an Irish dancer in Pennsylvania. This 'M' lady could still do her steps and she was pretty good, even though she appeared to be in her late thirties or early forties.

Liffey decided *definitely* not to tell her father that the 'M' lady had told her the letter 'M' on her necklace was the first letter of both her *first* and *last* names. Even though Liffey feared her father's brain was officially fried, he was not so feeble-minded as to *forget* that his wife's name was 'M'aeve 'M'cDermott.

"How old was my mother ten years ago when her plane crashed?" Liffey asked the large brown-eyed cow staring at her over a crumbling stone wall. "Is the diamond 'M' lady the right age to actually *be* my mother?" Liffey was three years old at the time of her mother's death and had no memory of the tragedy. She wished she could ask her father because he could give her the answer immediately. Something told her, however, that asking that question might send her despondent father into an even worse funk, so she and the cow had better figure this one out by themselves.

She tried to picture the Rivers' family Bible on the little tomb table at home. "Why can't I remember the *dates?*" Liffey thought irritably. Maeve McDermott's birth and death dates. Really *important* dates, but Liffey could not remember either of them now.

CHAPTER THREE

L iffey could no longer pretend that she was not starving to death. She had only eaten a few bites of trail mix since the Beltra Feis, and in the past eight hours, she had been through more emotional upheaval than most people experience in an entire lifetime.

She had made her first real friend, watched a tape that made her think her dead mother might not *really* be dead after all, solved the Queen Elizabeth I extra pearl mystery and climbed her first real mountain. To top things off, she had obviously ruined her relationship with her kind, wonderful father. "Quite a day's work," Liffey thought gloomily, trying not to become overwhelmed.

In spite of all of this, Liffey Rivers could not stop thinking about food and the Chinese restaurant she had seen in Strandhill earlier in the day. She doubted that her father had any appetite though, because he looked like a forlorn puppy stranded in the middle of a six-lane highway. She was genuinely surprised then, when her door lock popped up and she heard her father say the magic words: "Let's go find some shrimp fried rice, Liffey."

Liffey was thrilled that she was going to get to eat tonight, but also very concerned about her father. He was acting more like some kind of robot going through the motions than a flesh and blood parent.

"I love you, daddy. I'm so sorry I upset you so much on the mountain. I didn't mean to." "I know that, Liffey," Robert

Rivers answered sadly. Liffey knew he was thinking about her mother. So was she.

***

It was already after 9:30 p.m. and it was not yet completely dark. Liffey liked these long Irish days. She wondered if Irish children ever slept during them, or if they just faked it. She wished she had grown up in Ireland. She would have read thousands of books by now since the daylight here lasted until after 11:00 p.m. in the summers. In Wisconsin, she always had to sneak-read with a flashlight when her father ordered her to bed at 9:30.

The road winding down the mountain was more like a sidewalk *pretending* to be a road. It reminded Liffey of a twisty straw, and was so narrow, she was afraid they might not make it to the Chinese restaurant without side swiping another car or going off the road entirely. Robert Rivers' face was tranquil, but Liffey could see that his knuckles were chalk-white in the evening gloom. He was holding on to the steering wheel like a man dangling over a cliff. She admired him for not panicking, or at least not showing it if he *was* panicking. She shuddered looking down at Ballysadare Bay, far below, and the sheer drops from the edge of the road.

Liffey could not imagine how anyone *ever* learned to drive over here in Ireland.

CHAPTER FOUR

Mary Murphy tried to wake up from this latest installment of her recurring nightmare.

Her swollen body ached all over and she was barely able to swallow the mushy yams the hand with the big diamond ring offered her every few hours. Beautiful coal black women, wearing long white robes and veils, studied her through the doorway.

It was so very *hot* here. She must have a high fever. She might be dying. There was something about being terminally ill she seemed to recall. Maybe she was already dead and the white robed women were angels patiently waiting at the door until she was ready to leave with them?

There was also an old woman wearing an elaborately carved wooden mask on top of her head like a helmet. The mask grinned while the aged woman chanted in a high pitched voice and sponge fed a vile tasting liquid through Mary's parched lips.

It was so very, very hot here, wherever she was.

Whoever she was.

Always, the dream ended with a baby crying far away.

This dream cycle was taking its toll on Mary. She would wake up drenched with sweat and exhausted. Even more distressing than the nightmare, was the realization that she no longer felt safe with the man who said he was her brother.

She hoped that he had not noticed the doubt in her eyes. If he did, she would have to watch her step.

CHAPTER FIVE

The annoying 'Chicken Dance' alarm jolted Liffey out of a dreamless sleep, announcing shrilly that it was time to pack her bags and get ready for the long flight home.

Back to her boring, totally *pathetic* life in Wisconsin, and the sterile middle school prison where Principal Godzilla patrolled up and down the long corridors in his tweed jacket and squeaky athletic shoes. Worst of all, back to her Irish dance teachers who had a way of making Liffey feel like she was a waste of space.

"Daddy, do we *have* to go back today?" Liffey implored her rumpled father, who was sitting up in his bed staring straight ahead with a hollow expression.

"I *promised* Sinead we could see each other again before I had to leave!" Liffey begged.

"You *can* visit with Sinead. We don't have to leave for Dublin for another two hours," Robert Rivers replied. "You know, Liffey, Sinead is a remarkable young lady. She never left your side yesterday when things became so dangerous and confusing."

"I know. I think she's the nicest person I've ever met, daddy."

"Except for me of course," Robert Rivers smiled weakly.

"Well *obviously* except for you, daddy!"

***

"Did you *see* the news last night?

And look at the Dublin newspaper. *LOOK*!

You're on the *FRONT page*!" shrieked Sinead McGowan, waving the **QUEEN ELIZABETH I ATTENDS BELTRA FEIS** front page headline in Liffey's face and doing her utmost not to start screaming and jumping up and down with excitement.

"You're *famous*, Liffey! You were all over the *news* last night. You're a celebrity! We saw you on the telly in London outside the National Portrait Gallery with that *huge* crowd and all the police and even the Prime Minister! *Everybody* in Sligo is talking about you! But only a few of us from the Beltra Feis know your name and we're not talking! Although I cannot imagine *why* you want to remain anonymous! I'd be asking for a castle or something as a reward!"

"I might not even *be* here today if you hadn't taken such good care of me yesterday, Sinead," Liffey remarked.

"Well, what are friends for anyway?" Sinead laughed. "I have never had so much *fun* being terrified! It was like one of those adventures people have in the movies but it was really *happening!* I'd do it every day if we could!" "No you wouldn't," Liffey thought with a shudder.

Liffey tried hard not to think about leaving. Sinead McGowan was the only Irish dancer she had ever met at a feis who seemed to be there just to have fun. Meeting Sinead at the Beltra Feis was definitely the best time Liffey had ever had *anywhere.* Even though Liffey would be in the eighth grade this school year, something she had looked forward to since the sixth grade, thinking about going back to it now was very depressing.

She had no real friends at school. Just girls who were polite, but never sought her company and boys who were *total* idiots who thought slamming each other into the metal hall lockers was really funny.

Now that Liffey had *finally* met someone her own age, someone she totally connected with, she had to get back on a plane again in a few hours and disappear into the big black hole where she lived in Wisconsin.

***

After Liffey and Sinead had eaten their rashers and eggs at the little beach front cafe, Sinead suggested that they take a walk in the Strandhill sand dunes before Liffey and her father had to leave for the airport.

"Go ahead, girls, I'll be reading these Dublin and London newspapers for at least another hour," Robert Rivers said, sipping his third cup of coffee and nibbling on stale black pudding. He was pleased to note that the articles describing the Beltra Feis were mostly accurate and that the press had respected his wishes and kept his daughter's name out of their articles.

Watching Liffey and Sinead running out of the small restaurant, Robert Rivers was overcome with emotion. He had never seen Liffey so happy.

He thought again about Liffey's reaction to the videotape on the mountain last night and how things could not be normal again, until he had some kind of explanation as to the identity of the woman Liffey had met two years ago on that airplane.

Could it be *possible* that Liffey was right that it *was* Maeve sitting next to her on the plane? Then where has she *been*? And *who* was in the airplane that had blown up somewhere over the Atlantic ten years ago?

He stared out the cafe window at the surf breaking on the strand and the surfer lying on his board beyond the breakers, waiting for the perfect wave. He shook his head, and looked back at his *Irish Times*. No, it can't be. He had given up Maeve as lost years before.

But still, *could* it be possible…. He let the newspaper fall on the table and gazed back out at the silent Atlantic, remembering.

***

The three of them had traveled to Brazil where Maeve underwent treatment with a homeopathic doctor. When Maeve's health did not improve, she was referred to a private oncology clinic in Switzerland to treat the aggressive cancer which had been discovered in Chicago during routine pregnancy tests.

Robert Rivers and three-year-old Liffey boarded a regular flight to Zurich. Maeve was transported by a private hospital plane with medics and one other critically ill patient. Her plane had never arrived in Switzerland.

When a small, charred wing section of Maeve's plane washed ashore on the Ivory Coast of Africa, Attorney Rivers hired a recovery team to search for the wreckage of his wife's plane. But neither survivors nor plane had ever been found.

Could Liffey be right? Was she *really* sitting next to Maeve McDermott Rivers, her own *mother*, two years ago on that airplane headed for Seattle? Then where had Maeve *been for the last ten years*? Where was she *now*? It couldn't be. Robert Rivers took one last sip of his lukewarm coffee. He did not believe in ghosts.

Until now.

CHAPTER SIX

Mary Murphy checked her watch. There was barely enough time to make her flight to Chicago because she had overslept again after another night's troubled sleep. She gulped down the first three of nine pills she took each day, which, according to her brother, kept her alive. "No time for breakfast this morning," she announced to a box of unopened corn flakes sitting on the kitchen table next to an empty cereal bowl.

The formal reception for the International Diamond Exhibition was to begin at 8:00 p.m., Chicago time, and it was imperative that she arrive several hours beforehand to supervise setting up the booth.

The Seattle morning traffic was surprisingly light and Mary pulled into the long term airport parking lot with time to spare. She would have to try to get some sleep on the lengthy flight to Chicago.

While she waited to check in for her flight, she nervously twisted a delicate silver chain which held an exquisite diamond 'M' ornament, through her fingers. As usual, she had the overwhelming feeling that she did not really belong in the diamond trade business. She didn't like it. It felt 'wrong' to her, like she was living someone else's life. Donald told her that the diamond 'M' necklace she wore twenty-four hours a day had belonged to their mother, Maria Murphy. He said that their father, William Murphy, had given it to his bride as a wedding gift and that their mother had given it to Mary for her eighteenth birthday.

This background information had confused Mary and she asked Donald why he went by the name 'Smith' if their family surname was 'Murphy?' Donald looked taken aback and answered her question in one sentence: "It's a long story."

The first memory Mary had of her entire life-to-date, was her brother caring for her when she had been so desperately ill in Africa. If he had not found her there at the tiny Sisters of Charity hospital, she might *still* not know *anything* at all about her previous life, or for that matter, even *who* she was. She apparently owed everything to her brother who had searched for her when she went missing and brought her back to Seattle.

Mary could not understand then, *why* she had recently begun to be *afraid* of Donald. There was no real reason. It was just a strange feeling. Also, there was the fact that *every* single time over the last ten years she had asked him questions about her life before the amnesia, he was very evasive.

Could it be that there were horrible *secrets* he was keeping from her?

Things she had done that her brother wanted to shield her from?

Was she hiding from something? Or someone?

Why did she not have one *single* friend or relative? Someone who was thrilled she had recovered her health in Africa and had come home again?

Where were all the photographs? Donald told her that their parents were dead. He said they died fifteen years ago in a house fire which had destroyed everything they owned, including Mary's personal possessions which, according to Donald, she had been temporarily storing with their parents while she searched for a new apartment.

There *was* a photo of her in her high school yearbook. It was the only one she had from her past. Mary did not think she looked *anything* like the 'Mary Murphy' in that picture. The nose was wrong. It was too short. And her eyes were set further apart than they now were. People's eyes did not move *towards* their ears over time. They remained stationary.

And *how* did she end up in an *African* jungle?

Her brother told her she was traveling to South Africa to inspect diamond mines for their family business when she had suddenly become very ill.

Mary was afraid that she might have done something terrible in her past because otherwise, wouldn't there be *somebody* wanting to get to know her again? Had she *never* had a boyfriend or best girlfriend or cousins or aunts and uncles? What was *wrong* with her? Why was it like she had dropped off the face of the earth, even after she had returned to her supposed home?

***

When Mary struggled to remember events or people from her past, she always drew a complete blank. There were no specific memories, good or bad. But every so often, she would have a quick flash of recognition if she were watching or doing something and it seemed familiar. Like the time several years ago, waiting to change planes in Houston, when the thought occurred to her that she might have taken Irish dance lessons in her youth. She had eaten airport chili with the delightful little girl who was sitting next to her on the plane. When they returned to the gate area to re-board their flight to Seattle, she watched the young lady practicing her Irish dance steps.

She remembered showing the young lady how to improve her footwork and telling her that she might have taken Irish dance lessons too when she was young, even though she had no real memory of dancing Irish, or for that matter, any other way. Mary *could* remember how much she had liked that little girl and how it saddened her when they went their separate ways at the Seattle airport.

Mary smiled. *What* was the little girl's name? It was something unusual.

It had been after the encounter with the young Irish dancer that Mary had begun to sense something major was being kept from her. How she *wished* she could remember the little girl's name!

CHAPTER SEVEN

The flight from Dublin was on time. Robert Rivers looked down at Lake Michigan and Chicago's expansive gold coast skyline.

Liffey was fast asleep next to him and had been for the past five hours when exhaustion finally hit her like a sledgehammer.

He had spent most of his time on the long flight home trying to put together the jigsaw pieces of the most difficult puzzle of his life. How *could* there have been so much that had happened to them in such a short time period? It was like they had flown over the Atlantic Ocean directly into the Twilight Zone. Nothing made sense anymore. There was no black and white. Everything was grey.

***

Liffey was startled awake when the Aer Lingus plane dropped its landing gear. She *hated* that noise. It always sounded like the bottom of the airplane was falling off. Through the tiny window, she could see the little shamrock on the wingtip, and the shadow of the plane trailing along underneath them like Peter Pan chasing his shadow.

Before the mechanical noise woke her up, Liffey was in the middle of a pleasant dream. She was attached to a huge golden moon by a rope of moonbeams tied around her waist. It was pulling her up a rocky mountain path like she was water skiing.

This was the *second* time the moon seemed to be telling Liffey something. It was becoming apparent to Liffey that perhaps the moon *wanted* her back up on Knocknarea. The only question in her mind was *why?*

Liffey had learned in science class that nine-tenths of the human body is made up of water. Why might it not be *possible* then for the moon to be pulling on *her* small human body of water just like it pulled on the oceans, creating tides?

***

Liffey braced herself for the long walk to the baggage area. She was completely worn out and wanted to go back to sleep right now, even though it was only 3:45 p.m. It was six hours later in Ireland and her sleeping schedule was on Irish time now. After she and her father managed to pull their oversized luggage off the carousel, she thought about what lay ahead. One thing was for absolute certain. She did *not* want to go back to Wisconsin.

"Daddy, *let's stay* in Chicago tonight! We can get a room at the Palmer House Hotel and eat at that restaurant where they light the food on fire!"

Before Robert Rivers could object or even react, Liffey was thanking him in advance for the fun finale to their trip. Caught completely off guard, Robert Rivers sighed and agreed. "All right Liffey. We'll have one last night on the road. To tell you the truth, even though it's only a few hours away, I don't think I have the strength to drive back to Wisconsin tonight. I am completely out of gas."

YES!!! Liffey was *totally* elated. No Wisconsin tonight, but *most* importantly, no prison tomorrow! Her father had obviously forgotten that she was supposed to start back to school tomorrow morning bright and early at 7:30 a.m. and she did not remind him.

What kind of time *was that* to start a day anyway? Like it was even *possible* for anybody to stay awake! Like she could even *care* so early in the morning what any lame teacher had to say about anything.

Sinead said school in Sligo started at 9:15 each morning. Now *that* made sense. Kids ought to be *sleeping* at 7:30 a.m., not pretending to be awake sitting in school homerooms. And getting to school so early in the morning was *horrifying*. Liffey's father would leave for his Chicago law office at 6:30 a.m. each day. He would always make sure Liffey was wide awake before he left and depended on her to get on the school bus.

Liffey *hated* riding the school bus each morning because hers was usually the last bus to pull into the long school driveway. That meant she was usually getting inside the door just seconds before the noisy buzzer went off, warning students that they were *late* if they were not already sitting at their homeroom desks. It wasn't good enough to be standing *outside* their homerooms by their lockers. They had to be sitting at their desks facing the firing squad attendance taker *before* that buzzer went off. Or else!

Liffey never rushed into the school building from the bus like the other students, because her brain simply would not tell her feet to hurry so early in the morning. This meant that she routinely had to crawl on the floor past the front office to avoid being seen over the Dutch door by the staff who were on the phones listening to voicemail from parents about their sick kids who were not going to show up for classes that day. The school secretaries would record the absences as they peered out into the hallway, eagerly watching for students who were coming in late, so they could nail them with detentions and after school study halls.

Liffey had it down to a science. If she got through the front entrance doors when Godzilla was already broadcasting his stupid, totally *not* funny morning joke over the intercom, she would turn right and then immediately get down on all fours. It was always the same message. Godzilla would start warning students about all the horrible things that would happen to them if they *did* do this or did *not* do that. Like anybody was even listening.

After crawling past the office, Liffey would try hard to make her feet rush along the halls to her homeroom. If she was lucky, her homeroom teacher was preoccupied reading the morning newspaper and would not notice her slipping into her desk during the daily principal bombardment.

It was no wonder then that Liffey Rivers was thankful she had managed to negotiate one more day of freedom.

CHAPTER EIGHT

Mary's flight from Seattle was thirty minutes late when it landed at Chicago's O'Hare International Airport. This late arrival could be a real problem if she were not able to hire a cab immediately outside the crowded airport terminal. It was almost 3:45 p.m. and Monday's rush hour would have already begun.

She knew better than to cut things this close. There was only an hour and a half to get her suitcase and navigate through the crushing inbound traffic to the Chicago Loop.

Mary had deliberately taken the last flight from Seattle to Chicago. She secretly wished that her flight had been cancelled. Her brother would have been furious, but then she would be spared going through the motions, pretending she cared about the quality of their precious gems and the family business which she knew nothing about, except for what her brother had told her.

***

She managed to flag down a cab and tried to relax. Her attempt to catch up on lost sleep on the plane had not gone well. When she had finally closed her eyes and drifted off to sleep, there had been a new nightmare.

She was standing on top of a high mountain in front of an immense pile of rocks. There was a gigantic full moon. She was frantically looking for someone but she did not know who it was.

A little girl began to climb up the steep mountain, tiny arms stretched out, crying, "Mommy! Mommy! *Here* you are!" But when Mary extended her arms to embrace the little girl, there was no one there. Only what appeared to be clouds or fog. This sent Mary into a panic. She feared the little girl was lost on the mountain in the mist. She ran around frantically looking for the little one shouting, "Come back! Come back! I'm over here! I'm over here!" over and over, but the little girl had vanished.

Mary woke up in a cold sweat, trembling all over. The little girl had called her "Mommy!"

Was she a *mother?* If so, where was her child? Had she *abandoned* her? Even worse, had she *harmed* her child? Is *that* what her brother was trying to keep from her?

CHAPTER NINE

The Rivers' silver BMW was stuck in expressway traffic. "This is the downside of spending tonight in Chicago," Robert Rivers observed wryly, "sitting in endless traffic jams."

As their car inched its way towards the Loop, Liffey could not help thinking again about the dream she had on the flight back from Ireland. Could the *moon* really be trying to get her back up on the summit of Knocknarea?

Fully aware of how ridiculous this seemed, Liffey could not shake the feeling that she was *supposed* to climb that mountain again. She and her father had *just* returned *home* from Ireland. She could *hardly* ask him to turn around and go right back again because the *moon* wanted her up there! This would totally make her father think that *she* was the head case, when in fact it was her *father* who had been stretched way beyond *his* limits. He would tease her mercilessly and probably recite the 'Hey Diddle Diddle' rhyme about the cow jumping over the moon and the dish running away with the spoon every time he looked at her.

Liffey would have to hope that the moon did something spectacular again. Soon. Like an encore. Next time, if there *was* a next time, she would have to make sure her father saw it too. Otherwise, her chances of going back to Ireland in the near future to climb the mountain again were less than zero. She would keep the moon dream to herself for the time being.

***

The cab maneuvered slowly through the traffic on the in-bound Kennedy Expressway. Mary looked anxiously at her watch. There was just barely enough time to make it to the Palmer House before the diamonds arrived. "Isn't there some way you can just get us through all this traffic?" she implored the sullen, unpleasant driver.

"Sure. Thanks for reminding me about the traffic, lady. I'll just activate my rear end propellers and then we'll fly right over all these backed up cars."

"Sorry for asking," Mary replied meekly. The cab driver grunted.

The Sears Tower loomed into view and Mary breathed a sigh of relief. Not too much longer now. She stared idly at the cars and their passengers on either side of her. Unlike hers, the other two lanes were at least moving, although at half a snail's pace. She noticed the new metallic silver BMW crawling past her cab. "Definitely a boy toy," she thought, observing the handsome, forty-something man at the wheel.

Then she saw a young lady, who was probably his daughter, sitting next to him in the front passenger seat with her chin up, palms raised just above her shoulders as if in prayer or meditation. "Pretty sophisticated Zen stuff for someone that age," Mary observed.

It was when the BMW began to pull away in its unclogging traffic lane that Mary thought she recognized the front seat passenger. She looked a lot like that girl—*Liffey! That* was the name of the Irish dancer she had spent so much time with on the flight to Seattle from Pittsburgh! Only she looked older now. "I was just *thinking* about her this morning and here she is!" thought Mary happily, rolling down the back window of the cab and waving wildly, trying to get Liffey's attention.

The BMW was speeding off and probably a mile ahead of her when Mary's taxi finally began to disentangle itself from its lane, which was by far the slowest on the congested expressway. "I should have *walked*," Mary thought irritably, deeply regretting that she had missed the opportunity to connect again with *Liffey*, her young Irish dancer friend.

CHAPTER TEN

Liffey thought that arriving at the Palmer House Hotel under its canopy of blinding little lights was the best thing about staying there. It was like being a movie star arriving at a premiere. The doormen always treated her like royalty, so she began to act like it when her father brought her along with him on business trips to the elegant hotel.

When she had begun Irish dance lessons almost three years ago, Liffey created her own secret realm and became 'Princess Erin,' supreme ruler of an obscure kingdom off the west coast of Ireland where, by royal proclamation, her subjects did 'hop one-two-threes' and were forbidden to walk in a conventional manner. Walking was strictly taboo and punishable by, for the first offense, mandatory attendance at one of Liffey's Irish dance classes taught by an evil young woman who could make anyone feel dreadful and hopeless. Second time offenders were sentenced to watch the first one thousand dancers compete during the annual Midwest Oireachtas. There had never been any third time offenders because the punishment for the first two offenses was so severe.

'Princess Erin,' obeying her own royal decree, would do hop one-two-threes down the carpeted entrance into the hotel, chin lifted regally.

This time around, being thirteen and a bit more self-conscious about displaying her daydreams, she stuck her chin up, but only did her straight as a board 'I am an Irish dancer walk' gliding smoothly down the red carpet into the hotel lobby.

After 'Princess Erin' and her father checked into the Palmer House, they were too exhausted to do anything more than go to their room and hibernate. It was almost midnight in Ireland now, and sleep was overcoming both of them like Dorothy and her three friends in the poppy field.

"Let's eat dinner for breakfast tomorrow morning, daddy," Liffey suggested sleepily. "No objection, counselor," Attorney Rivers replied, trying unsuccessfully to stifle a big yawn.

**

Donald Smith looked at his altered appearance in the taxi's rearview mirror as it pulled away from Mitchell Airfield in Milwaukee. He hoped the hour and a half drive to the Chicago Loop would be uneventful. "Not bad," he said as he studied his new hair color. Mary would probably not notice he had dyed his brown hair black. The silver haired 'distinguished gentleman' look was completely gone now. Mary had never seen him disguised as 'Mr. McFleury.' He grinned, thinking how Mary noticed very little if she took her pills 'as prescribed' each day.

**

Mary arrived at the Palmer House with only thirty minutes to spare. She had never cut things this close before and was relieved she had pre-registered online and only had to pick up her room key. She needed to change her clothes and try to muster up some enthusiasm for the long night ahead.

Her room was small, but adequate. She parted the heavy, full length, blue drapes and looked down at the bumper to bumper traffic on the street three floors below. "How do people sit in all that traffic every day?" she wondered, hastily changing from her travel attire into a flattering apricot linen suit for the diamond show opening.

Mary thought again about the silver BMW and its occupants. She could not stop thinking that there was something familiar about not only the young girl, who she was 99% sure was *the* Liffey she had met two years ago, but also the man driving the car.

He was probably Liffey's father. Maybe he had been at one of the diamond conventions she routinely worked? After one of them was over, individual faces tended to melt together into a big collage. She thought it unlikely that she would have actually *met* Liffey's father and not remembered the occasion because he was a very handsome man.

What if she *had* met him before her illness robbed her of her memory? Might she finally have a *real* memory from her past?

***

Liffey thrashed about in the comfortable bed and could not believe she was unable to get back to sleep again. Her father was snoring loudly from his bed on the other side of the large hotel room.

"I should have never passed out on the trip over," she whispered to the shadow puppet she had made on the wall in the halo of light cast by the night lamp next to her bed. "That was totally stupid! What if I had to go to school tomorrow? I'd be snoring like daddy in homeroom." Calculating that it was already way past bedtime in Ireland, she put off texting Sinead for the moment. She laughed, remembering the funny burping sound Sinead's mobile made when it received incoming texts. She missed Sinead already. They had promised to keep in touch every day.

"I think I'll go for a walk around the hotel," Liffey decided. "And I am *not* going to wake up daddy and ask permission. He might start acting weird again and want to leave the hotel to test *Chicago* taxis out to see how they compare with the ones in Ireland and London. I am *not* going to risk that and have to ride all over Chicago tonight with him!"

"Besides, nothing can happen to me in a nice place like this," Liffey rationalized, quietly opening the door and slipping out into the gold-carpeted hallway.

***

Donald Smith glanced at his watch in the registration line at the Palmer House. It was 8:38 p.m. He was already late for the diamond show. "As the Irish would say, 'No worries,'" he thought. "Good old Mary will be all doped up and standing in place at the booth." By now, she would have already taken the second dose of her three-times-daily 'prescription pills.' The pills, he told her, which kept her alive.

The reality was, the pills made her sluggish and indecisive. They were designed to keep her under his thumb. Mary had never once crossed him. She was like a trained seal.

CHAPTER ELEVEN

Liffey did hop one-two-threes down the long plush corridor. On the way back to her room, she would practice her leap-overs and try to hold them longer.

Liffey knew that she had to practice a lot more if she were going to do well at the Fall Festival Feis, which was only a week from this coming Saturday. She needed a hard workout and major hornpipe help. She also knew she could not depend on her Irish dance teachers at Thursday night's dance class to correct the problems she had with her clicks. She usually missed her heels altogether when she tried to do a click. Therefore, Liffey was contemplating taking drastic action.

She would find a hand-held clicker that she could hide in her fist to make foot clicking sounds when her feet would at least get in range of each other. Then, if a feis judge *heard* the clicking sound, he or she might be fooled into thinking that they had blinked or sneezed and missed seeing her heels actually click together. It was worth a try. She was not at all sure if any of her own teachers could actually *do* these clicks themselves and she was absolutely *certain* none of them cared if Liffey Rivers, the invisible one, was doing them properly.

***

It was 8:45 p.m. when Donald Smith realized he was very jet lagged, even though he had slept for several hours on the flight from Belfast, anticipating this late night in Chicago.

He needed some coffee. An espresso. "Make that a double," he yawned, walking up to the coffee bar in the lobby.

He stared blankly into the lobby waiting for his brew, and was startled when an elevator door opened and a young girl leapt out into the hallway, quickly changing her peculiar arrival style into a normal gait.

There was something graceful, although rigid, about the way she strolled along like she had a board attached to her spinal cord. He groaned when he realized it was probably another Irish dancer. They all acted crazy. He had had his fill of them. Were they everywhere now? *Like bacteria?* He had hoped he would never see another Irish dancer again as long as he lived after the debacles in Ireland and St. Louis. An Irish dancer had cost him dearly at both places. If she ever turned up again, he would make sure that it would be the *last time.*

Enough was enough.

CHAPTER TWELVE

Liffey inspected the 'International Diamond Exhibition' sign at the end of the lobby. Diamonds had always intrigued Liffey. But when she flashed back to St. Louis and the solo dress crown on the porcelain Irish dancer doll, she decided she had seen enough diamonds for the time being. On the other hand, how often did she go anywhere where zillions of diamonds were just sitting around waiting to be gawked at?

It slowly dawned on Liffey that there was nothing to do in this palatial Chicago hotel except walk around if you didn't have any money on you. She could sit and stare at the elaborate ceiling frescoes in the sumptuous reception lounge, but that was for old ladies. A better idea presented itself. She *could* eat ice cream at the snack shop and charge it to her room.

Before Liffey made up her mind as to whether she should go for the ice cream, she was somewhat relieved to feel a wave of drowsiness overcoming her. Anyway, a dancer training for a feis should not stuff herself with ice cream just because she was bored and could not think of anything better to do.

Liffey reached a compromise between her desire to see the diamond show, or just to return to her room for more catch-up sleep. She *would* go to the diamond show but only to peek in the door. Then she would go back to her room and pass out. If it looked really interesting, she would ask her father for the admission money tomorrow morning and check it out then.

***

Donald Smith walked up to the booth draped in luxurious blue velvet. For strategic placement, Donald had reserved the second booth to the left of the entrance doors in the large exhibition room. Experience had taught him that people tended to walk by the first booth when they entered a show and would start actually looking when they reached the second booth. Not that he particularly cared who did or did not look at his diamonds. It was all about keeping up appearances.

Mary was, as expected, smiling cheerfully and answering questions from prospective customers. Two off-duty Chicago policemen stood at the back of the booth, eyes scanning the crowd for anyone who looked like they might be trouble. Donald greeted them with a polite nod.

Diamond necklaces shimmered like ice crystals on a smooth blanket of new fallen snow in the long display case. Underneath the jewels were tiny plastic ice cubes, back-lit by pulsing blue light bulbs, creating a stunning effect against the dark blue velvet backdrop. Donald was satisfied.

Mary was a natural salesperson. He wondered if she might be an even better one if he adjusted her medication dosage down tomorrow so that more of her bubbly personality could surface. But that would be too risky. There was always the possibility she might finally remember who she *really* was. Since he had *no* idea *who* she really was either, or where she had come from prior to being dumped on that dusty jungle runway ten years ago, he would let well enough alone for now.

***

When Mary's feverish body was removed from the small hijacked plane and discarded on the remote dirt landing strip hidden in a dense tropical rain forest between two shallow bays, he had taken pity on her. The soldiers had come out of the jungle like an army of ants headed towards a picnic basket. They boarded the hijacked plane, restraining the medical transport team in the event that hostages might come in handy. As previously arranged, Donald handed the diamonds over to the hijacker disguised as the other critically ill patient being transported on the plane.

Donald told one of the heavily armed jungle militants that he strongly objected to their callous treatment of this critically ill and obviously pregnant woman. The young insurgent spit on the ground and said sarcastically, in perfect English, "Please tell her we are very sorry for any inconvenience this unscheduled stop may have caused her if she regains consciousness." Then he climbed into the cockpit and pointed his automatic rifle at the terrified pilot.

Why could they not have taken the dying woman to their next destination where they were to refuel? It was a modern airport and several well-equipped hospitals were only minutes away from it. They could just have easily abandoned her there. As things turned out, there had not been a 'next' destination, because the small plane had exploded off the coastline of the Canary Islands. There was a rumor among Donald's diamond associates that a lone parachutist had ejected from the plane just seconds before the explosion and had vanished without a trace. So did the diamonds.

Donald was pleased now that he had helped Mary recover her health because she had unwittingly become an integral part of his international smuggling network after he had provided her with a passport and new identity.

He had also made a nice little commission when he sold her newborn baby boy to the childless couple in South Africa. One day he might have to get rid of Mary. But not yet. As long as she remained clueless, she was very useful to him.

CHAPTER THIRTEEN

Robert Rivers woke up thirsty at 9:00 p.m. He had neglected to drink water prior to, or during the long flight back to Chicago from Dublin. Now he was dehydrated and restless.

He switched on his bedside light and quietly walked across the room to get a glass of water. He did not want to wake Liffey. She needed all the sleep she could get after their draining ordeal in Ireland.

When he checked in with his office in the morning, he would assign a staff investigator to coordinate with Interpol. The art thief could be anywhere by now and would most likely no longer look anything like the elderly gentleman 'winking' judge from the feis in rural Ireland, or the leather-jacketed smuggler Liffey referred to as the 'Skunk Man' in St. Louis. Attorney Rivers was certain that this man was a master of disguise. Liffey had only recognized him in Ireland as being the same man who had chased her in St. Louis, when he glued his dark eyes on her before she began her Jig.

Since Liffey had twice thwarted this obviously powerful and resourceful criminal, Attorney Rivers feared for his daughter's safety. He knew from his own clientele that some criminals became obsessed with avenging themselves on those they considered to be their enemies. Although Robert Rivers had managed so far to keep her name out of the news, a connected underworld character could easily learn her identity and address.

Liffey was wrong when she thought that her father had forgotten about school the next day. He wanted to make a few arrangements first. It would be necessary to secure the school building each morning before classes began until this man was apprehended.

As he gulped down the much needed water, he could not help thinking that it was almost unbelievable that Liffey and McFleury, the Skunk Man, or whoever he really was, kept crisscrossing paths. What were the odds? It was like a bad plot in a book. Who would even believe it? It all seemed absurd.

On the way back to bed to get what he hoped would be a few more hours sleep, he glanced over at Liffey's bed. She normally slept fitfully, tossing and turning, but he had not heard a sound.

The bed was empty.

He ran to the bathroom. It too was empty. Forcing himself not to imagine the worst, he hurriedly dressed and went out into the long hallway towards the bank of elevators. If she was not snacking downstairs at the 24-hour cafe, he would alert the hotel staff, and then the Chicago Police if it came to that.

CHAPTER FOURTEEN

Liffey strolled along the short corridor leading to the diamond exhibition. Inside the conference hall, she could see groups of well dressed people standing around the diamond displays. Many of them were throwing their heads back, laughing boisterously. Liffey thought they seemed to be trying too hard.

Some of them were sipping champagne, which was being offered by waiters walking around in tuxedos. Other waiters glided along with plates of hors d'oeuvres casting delicious aromas her way, making Liffey ravenous. She knew that it was her own idea to skip dinner tonight, so she couldn't blame anyone but herself.

She spotted a table right inside the door heaped high with mini tacos. They smelled so good, that her stomach's 'feed-me-now' impulse was beginning to replace her self-control. She forgot all about the $15.00 entrance fee and smiled at the ticket takers as she sailed right by them. They smiled right back.

Liffey went straight for the food. She pretended to admire a gold embossed Palmer House china plate and then began to quickly pile on the Mexican food. There were bowls of guacamole and salsa surrounded by mountains of tortilla chips. "This is *heaven*," Liffey thought, practically inhaling a taco while she dipped into the bowl of guacamole with a colorful red and orange pottery spoon.

Eventually, she remembered her manners, and how it was not polite to cram food into your mouth faster than you could chew it. Liffey forced herself to slow down a bit and daintily dipped a tortilla chip into the guacamole on her plate. Then she casually nibbled on it, just in case there were undercover food bouncers watching for people like her.

Since Liffey was now more-or-less a non-paying guest of the International Diamond Exhibition, she figured she might as well have a look around. She decided she would begin on her left, curve to the right, and then exit when she had made her way back to the entrance.

The first booth she came to had two nervous-looking bald men standing behind the display case. They gave her an unmistakable 'get lost kid' look while she munched on her pile of chips. "I guess they don't see any dollar signs above my head," Liffey thought. She didn't blame the bald men because it was obvious that she was not there to buy diamonds tonight. She stepped aside and let a bushy-haired man take her place, thinking, "Maybe he can trade them some of his hair for one of their pretty rocks."

The next booth had a big crowd around it. Maybe that was why the bald men in the neighboring booth had such a sullen look about them. They reminded Liffey of the idiot boys at her school, and how they would give you hostile looks when you refused to let them eat *your* dessert after they had already devoured their own. If you told them to go away, they would sulk and often get into 'physical altercations' as Principal Godzilla referred to their stupid fights.

Liffey had experienced a physical altercation with a lunchroom moocher boy last year. She threw cold melted cheese sauce all over him when he started a tug of war over a brownie and then *she* got into trouble with Godzilla. It had not been at all fair, and Liffey determined after that lunchroom day, she would *never* again let a boy within ten feet of her while she ate. So she usually ate lunch alone because most of the girls wanted to flirt with the stupid boys rather than sit with Liffey Rivers, who was prepared to defend her desserts even if it meant another trip to Godzilla's office.

Liffey continued worming her way through the throng, imagining how spectacular the diamonds at the next booth must be to have such a large crowd waiting to see them. When Liffey finally made it to the front of the group, she was stunned by the unearthly current of blue light pulsing through the intertwined diamond necklaces.

This display was almost as exciting as viewing the Royal Crown Jewels at the Tower of London. Liffey was *thrilled* and could feel one of her solo dress trances coming on.

There she was, doing her Slip Jig in her new blue dress. Only this time, the dress was drenched with tiny little diamonds sparkling like shooting stars as she moved effortlessly around the stage. She looked like a comet streaking through the sky!

Liffey was completely oblivious to everyone and everything around her except the blue diamonds and her starry solo dress until an excited voice broke through her hypnotic state.

"Liffey??? I can't *believe* it! I saw you on the expressway today and *here* you are! How *wonderful* it is to see you again! Stay *right* there! I'll take a break in a few minutes and we can visit properly. I can't *wait* to hear how your Irish dancing is coming along. Is that hornpipe still giving you so much trouble? Just give me a minute. *Don't move!* I'll turn things over to my brother here and be right with you. Stay *right* where you are. We'll go and find some chili!"

Liffey turned her head towards the familiar voice and locked eyes with a beautiful woman who was wearing a diamond

'M' necklace. Liffey tried hard to focus on what was happening here, but didn't believe it *could* be happening. She must have walked into a parallel universe like in a science fiction movie or something because this was just too freaking weird.

The only rational explanation would be that she was still up in her hotel room and sound asleep and that this was all just a dream. A *wonderful* dream. Was she actually looking into the deep blue eyes of her *mother?* If that was who the diamond 'M' lady really was? Liffey did not want to wake up!

Her feeling of exaltation was short lived, however, because now the dream turned ugly and became her worst nightmare, when, directly behind the lovely diamond 'M' lady, the Skunk Man emerged from behind a curtain. He stared hard at her with his beady little eyes. She fully expected his tongue to shoot out of his gross mouth like a lizard looking for bugs for its dinner.

Even though Liffey could not be sure if he recognized her without her Irish dancing curls, she nonetheless felt her blood leaving her brain and heading towards her feet. She knew now that she *had* to be dreaming. There was no way on this earth that her *mother*, if it *was* her mother, *and* the Skunk Man could be standing *together* in Chicago at this diamond exhibition!

And had Liffey heard correctly? Had the diamond 'M' lady called the disgusting Skunk Man her **BROTHER????**

Liffey decided it was time to wake up from this bizarre dream.

"Enough," she mumbled, shaking her head back and forth politely. "No thank-you, not now. I've had quite enough," she said to no one in particular, in a sing-song voice, like Alice in Wonderland declining the Mad Hatter's tea. She turned away from the phantoms, handed her plate of tacos to the startled young woman standing next to her, and quickly navigated back through the crowd, out into the hallway. She was doing her utmost to snap out of this deep, troubling sleep.

This dream, however, would not *quit*, and continued on now with her *father* making an entrance. Was he going to announce to her now that *he* was related to the Skunk Man too? Maybe the Skunk Man was actually her *real* father and Robert Rivers had kidnapped her from the hospital nursery shortly after birth.

Her father, if he really *was* her father, was dressed in sweats and calling to her from an elevator just outside the 'kingdom of the blue diamonds' where Liffey's mother and the repugnant Skunk Man lived.

"Daddy, I *need* to wake up! *Please, please help me wake up!*" she pleaded, as Robert Rivers ran up to her and gently led his dazed daughter back towards the elevators. "Of course I will help you wake up, Liff. I promise. But first, let's get you upstairs and back into bed. Looks like you've been sleepwalking."

That was IT! That *had* to be it! That was the *logical* explanation for this whole crazy scene. She was *sleepwalking!* In the morning, she and her father would have a big laugh over how ridiculous it was to have had this preposterous nightmare about running into the diamond 'M' lady, who was consorting with the Prince of Darkness himself in back of a diamond display case at a hotel in Chicago.

Robert Rivers would probably tell Liffey that all she needed was to get her subconscious brain flushed out, like he flushed the old oil out of his car engine when it got gooey. Then she would not have so many distorted images sloshing around in her poor head that caused grotesque nightmares like this one.

Liffey needed tomorrow to be here *soon* so she could wake up and go to the diamond show, just like she was thinking she would do tonight, before she fell asleep and this absurd dream had begun.

***

Robert Rivers gently tucked Liffey in under the soft, fleecy covers. This kind of sleepwalking had happened before. Twice in the past six months he had found Liffey wandering around their Wisconsin home in the middle of the night. But she had *looked* like she was sleepwalking then, babbling in gibberish with unseeing eyes. Tonight, she looked haunted. Like someone who had just seen their pet dog get run over by a car. And she spoke coherently tonight as well—in *complete* sentences.

The other scenario, that Liffey *did* see the diamond 'M' lady and had *not* been sleepwalking, was *impossible,* and he certainly could not risk leaving Liffey here alone in this hotel room in her fragile condition to go out chasing shadows. Years of practicing law had taught him to be practical and not to have unrealistic expectations.

CHAPTER FIFTEEN

Mary Murphy asked her brother to work the booth alone when she thought she spotted the delightful little Irish dancer she had met two years ago standing in the large crowd in front of their booth.

"*What* name did you call her, Mary?" Donald asked coldly.

"I think her name is 'Liffey,'" Mary began. "But I don't know her last name. I forgot to ask her before we went our separate ways. And to be honest, her first name might be something else. My memory is not exactly reliable. But I am pretty sure it is Liffey. I do remember for certain that she was on her way to Seattle for an Irish dance competition."

Donald snapped his quick decision right back at Mary. "Sure. I'll cover for you, Sis. You go and have a nice visit with your little friend and make *sure* to find out who she *really* is and especially *where she lives*. You wouldn't want to lose touch with her again," Donald said urgently. "Make sure you get her *home street address*. We might want to send her our Christmas card with the diamond Star of Bethlehem."

Mary rolled her eyes as she left the booth. This diamond sales life was getting to her. She was sick of thinking about them and pretending that they interested her.

Not only was she bored with this life, she was also paid very poorly by her brother who told her that her prescription pills alone cost him more than his house payment did each month.

Donald was on the road most of the time and when he *was* at home, he talked on his cell phone all day long and often made airline reservations to exotic places. It seemed like *he* was always on vacation somewhere and *she* was always house sitting in Seattle. They led totally separate lives. The big difference was he at least *had* a life. She did not, and was usually too exhausted to work on getting one.

Some days, when her brother was traveling, she stayed in bed until dinner time. Then she would get up, eat a slice of toast and climb right back into bed again. She had recently noticed that she *did have* the stamina to get through a day when her brother was at home with her, or when they were on the road together, like tonight. Mary had begun to suspect that he might be manipulating her prescription pills which would explain why she was usually in bed sleeping all day when Donald was gone.

Right now, she was anxious to find Liffey and pick up where they had left off. There was some kind of electromagnetic connection between them, as if they were tuned in to each other like old best friends. She knew this was a bit odd, considering she was way beyond old enough to be Liffey's mother, but there was something unusual happening here. For some reason, she cared deeply about this girl named 'Liffey' but had no idea why. It was amazing that their paths had crossed again so soon. Was it luck or fate?

***

Mary excitedly searched the crowd for Liffey for forty-five long minutes. Liffey had completely disappeared. Trying to hide her bitter disappointment from her brother, she was shocked and confused when he was *angry* about the mix-up and *blamed* her!

"Why did you *let* her get *away?*" he shouted. "You should have moved faster. She's only a kid. Five *minutes* of waiting for a kid is like five *hours* for an adult."

Mary turned away with tears in her eyes and a big lump in her throat. She felt like she had just lost something precious. A little tremor went through her. *Why* would her brother care one way or another about her reunion with Liffey anyway? "What's it to *him?*" she muttered under her breath, disturbed and confused by the twisted, cruel look she saw on his face.

CHAPTER SIXTEEN

It was 6:00 a.m. and Liffey was still sleeping soundly. Robert Rivers hoped she would wake up eager to eat breakfast like her old self again. He was worried about her. Last night's strange sleepwalking incident was a sign that she was in a very precarious mental state. At 8:00 a.m. he would call Sam Snyder and put him on Liffey surveillance, alternating with Margaret Williams, the newest detective on his staff of six investigators and fifteen attorneys. He would stop by his office before returning to Wisconsin and announce the reassignment news himself. He knew that Liffey had only been sleepwalking last night, but that did not change the fact that the man who might harm his daughter was out there somewhere.

Sometimes, Attorney Rivers thought he needed more full time investigators. The Rivers Law Firm specialized in criminal law and the detective staff did all of the preliminary fact finding for the attorneys. There would be an outcry when he removed the already over-worked Sam and Margaret and put them on Liffey bodyguard assignment. "This is one of the many benefits of owning your own business," he thought. "You can reassign manpower and nobody will say a word to your face. They will just gripe among themselves."

***

The huge orange moon began spinning above the mountain like a giant pinwheel. Liffey was terrified as it began to pulse spasmodically, like a beating heart ripped out of someone's chest, and began to free-fall towards her. Before she could scream, the scene switched to her as a little girl. She looked like she did in the photo with her mother and father by the lilacs when she was three years old. She was running towards the diamond 'M' lady, who was standing on top of the mountain extending her arms out to embrace her. Just as she reached the lady and held out her chubby little arms to hug her, the lady went up in a poof of smoke and Liffey began to cry, heartbroken.

***

Robert Rivers thought he heard muffled sobs as he splashed on the Bay Rum aftershave his daughter had given him last Christmas.

Liffey was sitting up in bed wiping away her tears when he reached her. Even though he reassured her that he would not let anything happen to her, he felt more like he was trying to convince himself. He did not know how to tell Liffey how concerned he was that there might be a retaliation attack by the international jewel and art thief whose agendas she kept ruining by some quirk of fate.

He hoped that when they returned home, the presence of a detective would prevent Liffey from looking over her shoulder each time she left the sanctuary of their well secured lake house. He knew that she had an upcoming feis and assured her that a detective would accompany her to the competition, along with himself and her Aunt Jean. Liffey groaned, remembering the last time she went to a feis with her aunt who had acted like an escapee from a lunatic asylum.

"Aunt Jean told me she has a big surprise for you Liffey, but she would not tell me what it was. She only said it had to do with Irish dancing and was very mysterious about it." Liffey burst out laughing and said, "*Anything* Aunt Jean does is mysterious, daddy. She is *certifiable!*" Secretly, Liffey still planned to talk with her eccentric Aunt Jean about Robert Rivers' obsession with taxicab testing.

"Bizarre Aunt Jean is all I've got," Liffey thought.

Just as she was deciding when would be a good time to call her aunt, Robert Rivers chimed in. "Why don't you get dressed quickly, Liff and we can grab a cab over to that pancake house you like so much?"

"*Here we go again!* Like I don't already have *enough* problems to deal with! I *have* to get daddy off this cab thing. It is *totally* weird and I am getting sick and tired of being dragged in and out of taxis just so he can compare them with each other. Why on *earth* would anyone even want to do this stupid taxicab analyzing thing?"

Instead of honestly telling her father that she could not endure any more of his cab rides, she decided to patronize him one more time and said, "Daddy, I would really *love* to go out grabbing cab rides all day long with you, but I stuffed myself full of tacos and guacamole last night in my blue diamond dream and I'm honestly not the least bit hungry right now."

Liffey hoped her 'no appetite' declaration might put off the inevitable cab ride for a bit longer. She was very surprised then, when all the color drained from her father's face and he emphatically said, "Liffey, it was just a *dream!* You are *always* ravenous in the morning and we did not even eat dinner last night because we both were too jet lagged and sleepy. You have GOT to be *starving* by now! I would expect that by this time you would be happy to eat your bedspread!"

"Well, I'm *really* sorry, daddy, but I'm just *not* hungry. Maybe snacking in your dreams fills you up?" she said with a little laugh, hoping to stimulate her father's sense of humor. Liffey knew that Robert Rivers did not normally eat a big breakfast like she did each morning, and that he was only suggesting the pancakes for her sake.

"Why don't you run down to the cafe and get yourself some toast and bacon?" she suggested. "I'll stay here and watch cartoons."

"*Cartoons?*" thought Robert Rivers. "Liffey will watch *cartoons* instead of *eating pancakes?*" Liffey's father knew that she seldom watched *any* television, let alone cartoons. She hadn't watched *morning* cartoons since she was eight.

"I think I'm just going to order room service then," Robert Rivers said quietly. "Would you like anything to drink, Liffey?"

"Just tea, please, daddy," she answered happily, thinking that in a few more hours it would be time to call her friend Sinead in Sligo.

***

That did it! Liffey only wanted tea! It slowly dawned on Robert Rivers that his daughter had no interest in eating breakfast for the first time in her life. Instead of calling room service, he went into the bathroom and dialed his staff detective on call. When a pleasant young man answered, "This is Sam," Attorney Rivers said: "Sam, this is Robert Rivers. I need you to come immediately to the Palmer House. It's an emergency. My daughter Liffey will not eat breakfast and is in grave danger. I will meet you at the elevator bank on the 4th floor so I can watch our room from the hallway while we talk. Please call me when you are in the lobby."

"Yes, Sir, I'll be there in thirty minutes or sooner depending on traffic," Sam answered politely, trying not to laugh and blurt out what was really on his mind: "Are you *kidding*? That's a first! Your daughter skips breakfast and *that* means she's in grave danger? Get a clue here Attorney Rivers, she's probably on a diet," he laughed, inspecting the month and date on his watch. Was this an April Fool's Day joke in September?

"Good," Robert Rivers replied, terminating their short conversation.

CHAPTER SEVENTEEN

Mary telephoned Donald's hotel room to tell him that she had a terrible migraine headache and would be late getting to the booth this morning, if she could manage to get there at all.

He was not amused. She promised him that she would come as soon as her pain medication kicked in and she could stand up again without feeling dizzy.

Mary reached for the large pill container on the bed stand next to her and located the 'Week 4-Monday' pill compartment in the 31-day dispenser.

Then she walked into the bathroom, broke each of this Monday's pills in half and dumped the other halves in the toilet and flushed them down. She had not taken any of last night's 'go to bed dose.' She realized now she had made a mistake because her head felt like it had crashed through a brick wall. She needed to get some medical advice about how to withdraw from her prescriptions. The problem was that she had no idea *what* she was taking and Donald had told her he got the pills from a South African pharmacy! He said they were custom made and were designed just for her by a tropical disease clinic in Egypt.

In spite of her misgivings about what withdrawing from these pills might bring upon her, Mary had made up her mind to find out what life would be like without them. Her aching head was the result of the first missed dose. She hoped it did not get too much worse than this because she decided she was only going to take half a dose this morning. She would then slowly withdraw from all the pills. She knew she had to try.

Her brother's very hostile behavior yesterday, after she had failed to locate the little girl in the crowd, unnerved Mary this morning as much as it had last night. It just did not make *any* sense. *Why* would Donald care the *least* little bit that she had been unable to find Liffey? It was not like him to be interested in *anything* she did, unless it involved his diamonds. And why would a reunion she hoped to have with a *child* she had met on an airplane two years ago be of any interest to him at all?

Some kind of sixth sense she did not even know she possessed until last night was telling her that her brother *knew* who that child was, and wanted to know where she lived so that he could *harm* her in some way. She knew this seemed insane, but something stirred deep within her, like she had always imagined a maternal instinct would be like if your child was in danger. She did not understand this urgent feeling to protect Liffey which was surging through her, but she intended to act upon it.

Her first step would be to secretly wean herself off all her medications. She had had her doubts about them for several months. Mary suspected they might be downers because she felt dull and drained of energy almost all of the time. "Mirror, mirror on the wall, who's the dullest of them all?" Her bathroom mirror answered each time, "You are." She also thought it was very suspicious that her brother always doled the pills out to her himself like she was a child.

If she did die like her brother said she would if she stopped taking the pills, then so be it. She was already pretty much dead anyway and she was willing to take the risk that he was lying to her. Mary somehow knew that it was vitally important to keep her wits about her from this moment on.

CHAPTER EIGHTEEN

Donald Smith was very much put out that Mary had called his room to report she had a migraine. He had counted on her manning the display booth this morning while he met with his Chicago syndicate to set up their next 'project.' Now he would have to reschedule and bump it up to later this afternoon.

He also had intended to start searching for the 'Liffey' girl to put an end to her interference with his professional life. *Two* fiascos because of a little brat! It was enough to make him crazy, and he was going to make sure that it did not happen a third time.

Donald had taken great care to significantly alter his appearance today. If anyone were looking for him, they would never guess he was both the elderly Irish feis judge *and* the punk guy in St. Louis. He was wearing thick eye glasses now with black frames. One of his arms was 'replaced' with an artificial prosthetic device because he had 'lost his arm in a serious accident.' There was no similarity to either of the disguises the Irish dancer had seen him use. If she came back to the booth today, she would not recognize him. Then he would make his move. There was a different security crew on duty today, so he would not raise eyebrows when he arrived at the booth in his new attire.

"Teens often experiment with drugs and sometimes accidentally overdose," he reflected. It would be relatively simple to arrange such a thing here in Chicago where he was so well connected.

If he himself was unable to take care of things, his associate, who was stationed outside the hotel's front door, would be on her trail immediately. Between the two of them, the odds were good that they would find her and there were many ways to make accidents happen.

He had done it before.

CHAPTER NINETEEN

While Robert Rivers waited for a phone call from the lobby, he considered the possibility of bringing Louise Anderson in from St. Louis where she had recently opened her own detective agency. He was concerned that his own staff was already overworked and Liffey still talked about Louise and how grateful she was for Louise's help at the Celtic Arch Feis earlier in the summer. While Sam and Margaret were very capable people, it was important that Liffey feel safe. He knew that if Louise was back at her side, it would make things easier for Liffey because she trusted Louise.

***

Sam Snyder waited by the elevators. His employer was walking slowly towards him down the hallway like an old man. Sam was startled to see how drained Robert Rivers appeared to be after his 'vacation' to Ireland. Attorney Rivers looked five years older than he had before his trip. "Maybe it's because his daughter really is at risk," Sam thought nervously.

After a briefing, it was decided that Liffey was not to be out of sight at any time and that Robert Rivers would go to the diamond exhibition to see if he recognized the diamond 'M' lady or her 'brother.' Sam would be introduced to Liffey as a prospective attorney that her father wanted to interview confidentially for a position with his firm. Liffey would buy that. Then Attorney Rivers would make a call and say he had to leave for twenty minutes. Liffey would be safe with Sam while he ventured downstairs and paid $15.00 to enter the 'land of the blue diamonds.'

***

Robert Rivers was barely able to breathe as he waited in the long line at the entrance to the International Diamond Exhibition. His heart was pounding. His legs were rubbery. If the diamond 'M' lady *was* in there at the booth with the blue diamonds, then he would simply make small talk and somehow manage to ask her if she had ever flown from Pittsburgh to Seattle. After a long career of attending obligatory social functions, Robert Rivers was able to converse effortlessly with anyone.

He did not dare to hope that it really *could* be his wife, Maeve, beyond those doors. Liffey *had* to have been mistaken about her assertion that the woman on the plane two years ago was the *same* woman she had watched briefly on the videotape.

In retrospect, he thought that he really should have asked Liffey to watch more of that tape. She had only seen the first thirty seconds, if that. Then he had quietly put it away. When he had the courage, he would ask her to watch it again with him and see if she still insisted that she had met Maeve on a plane two years ago.

Liffey had always been impulsive and prone to jump to conclusions. On the other hand, she had often exhibited amazing extrasensory perception. Sometimes he was sure she was psychic. That is why he had not completely discounted her when she was so adamant that her mother in the videotape was the diamond 'M' lady she had met while traveling to Seattle. He was not at all sure he would be able to rely on his legs remaining underneath him if the woman inside really *was* Maeve. He felt like a glob of jello out of its mold.

***

Robert Rivers walked slowly into the imposing gold and white ballroom which had been transformed into an elegant setting for the thousands of diamonds on display. He remembered the occasion when he and Maeve had attended a wedding reception in this same room. It had been the day after the good news that Maeve was expecting their second child.

He began his search and immediately located the booth with the 'blue' diamonds. This discovery sent a chill down his spine. *How* could Liffey have *known* about these diamonds if she had been dreaming? It was true that he had found her in the hallway next to the entrance doors, but she could not possibly have gotten in and then *out* the door again while she was sleepwalking, could she? It was a ticketed event and she did not have the 'get in the door' money. Had Liffey actually *been* in this room? He tried not to appear too unnerved as he walked up to the pulsing blue lights display case and pretended to admire the beautiful diamond necklaces.

He was both relieved and disappointed that there was no diamond 'M' lady standing behind the booth, only two security guards and a middle-aged man wearing a baggy blue suit. The man wore thick eyeglasses and had an artificial left arm. Robert Rivers considered engaging the salesman in conversation to find out if there was a woman who worked with him who wore a diamond 'M' necklace, but a gut feeling told him that this would not be a wise move, and he instead asked the man a question about the third necklace from the right.

"I am so sorry, sir. My lovely sister would be the one to give you the fine details as to this particular piece but she is indisposed with a headache this morning. I expect her to report in after lunch at 2:00 p.m."

Trying not to cry out, as it registered that Liffey was apparently *also* correct about a woman being part of this booth and that he now might actually be chatting with the Skunk Man, aka Donald McFleury, in yet *another* one of his disguises, Robert Rivers somehow managed to reply, "Great, I will definitely come back then. I am very interested in this piece."

"Good. We will expect you then at 2:00 p.m. May I ask your name?"

Did Robert Rivers imagine a glint of suspicion in the little rat-like eyes hidden behind the thick eyeglasses? He could not be sure.

"My name is Barker," Robert Rivers said unconvincingly. "Bob Barker."

CHAPTER TWENTY

L iffey was sick of babysitting this Sam guy who had turned up out of *nowhere* to be interviewed by her father. She thought Sam was pretty lame. When she had politely asked him what kind of law he liked best, knowing full well that her father's firm specialized in criminal law, Sam had answered: "I think I like tax law the most. It is always a challenge helping people take the maximum number of deductions they are entitled to take. Most people miss the most obvious ones. I find it very rewarding when they end up getting a refund from the government, rather than owing money to the Internal Revenue Service."

Liffey thought "Whatever," but courteously replied, "Well that's *very* interesting." They had nothing at all to talk about after that, so Liffey went back to watching *Rugrats*.

Sam kept looking out the window and then walking across the room and listening at the door like he heard someone or something out there. He was totally weird and acted like a nervous wreck. Liffey was beginning to think the entire world was full of nervous wrecks, herself included.

***

Robert Rivers returned to the room before Angelica outsmarted Chuckie again. Liffey clicked off the TV and turned Sam over to her father. "Sam says his *favorite* kind of law is doing people's *taxes*, daddy."

She hoped her father would get her drift. You couldn't tell anymore what he would do or say. It was like a universe gone mad lately everywhere she turned.

"Liffey," Robert Rivers was using his boring history lecture tone and she feared she might have triggered some kind of income tax monologue, "Sam Snyder is not a criminal defense attorney."

"Really?" Liffey replied. She wondered if he had even *heard* her telling him about the tax thing.

"Really," Robert Rivers replied. "Sam is here to protect you, Liffey. He is one of the firm's detectives." Sam gave Liffey a serious 'your father is absolutely right' nod like she was two or something. "Why do I need Sam to protect me?" Liffey asked, turning away from nodding Sam and aiming a 'you have *got* to be kidding' look at her father.

"Because you have somehow managed to undermine two sophisticated criminal networks, Liffey, and it is logical to think that there will be consequences. Anyone who was really looking hard for you would find you eventually. It's only a matter of time. We have to assume you are in danger until the man you have thwarted twice now is picked up by the authorities. You have wounded his ego and most criminals have huge ones. He will be after you if not sooner, then later."

A stab of uneasiness went right through Liffey from head to toe. She honestly had not considered that there might be repercussions. Suddenly her stomach was beginning to rearrange itself like it was being blended in a food processor. Her hands felt clammy and she felt all prickly and flushed when she blurted out: "I *wasn't* dreaming last night, daddy! I'm *still* full from eating so much! The Skunk Man *is* downstairs at the diamond show and the diamond 'M' lady is there too. *How* could she be his *sister*? Creatures like him don't *have* brothers or sisters, they have pet *tarantulas*. And *how* can my path keep crossing over his? It's like a higher power keeps thrusting us together against *both* of our wills! Like I am *supposed* to be bumping into that jerk everywhere I go. I just don't *get* it. It's not fair! I'm only thirteen, so how much bad karma could I have? "

"If karma is real, then the Skunk Man will get what is coming to him someday, Liffey," said Robert Rivers.

"And if the diamond 'M' lady *is* my mother, then obviously the Skunk Man is *not* her brother because she was an only child," added Liffey. "Why then would she *pretend* that *he was* her brother? Nobody in their right mind would...."

Liffey felt like a cat arching its back when it sees a large dog coming at it. The little invisible hairs on the back of her neck stood up on end.

Nobody in their right mind...

CHAPTER TWENTY-ONE

One thing experience had taught Donald Smith was that he knew when it was time to go. Even though he intended to put an end to the Irish dancer's meddlesome behavior, his first priority was to protect himself and his diamond network and he was certain that this 'Mr. Barker,' or whoever he *really* was, did not want to look at a necklace again at two o'clock. The transparent Mr. Barker wanted something else and Donald was not going to wait around to find out what it was. Donald had detected a 'big trouble' vibe from Bob Barker. There was also the disturbing fact that 'Mr. Barker' looked vaguely familiar.

Donald Smith would have to delegate the Liffey problem to one of his Chicago colleagues. His man at the front door would do. His fees were reasonable and he always finished the job without a trace left behind.

Right now, Donald needed to get security organized to make a show of moving the diamonds from the hotel and out to the airport by armored car. There were several 'sales' that were to have closed this afternoon but "that's just too bad," he smirked. Selling diamond necklaces was only a front. A way to appear legitimate as he routinely moved millions of dollars worth of diamonds from his illicit headquarters in Africa. He told the diamond exhibition committee that there was a serious family emergency he had to deal with immediately and that he and his sister would be taking a 3:30 flight to Miami. Instead,

Donald booked a 1:30 flight to Houston where he needed to take care of something important.

***

Mary reacted to her brother's news that they must immediately leave the hotel and return to Seattle, with disbelief and anger, a reaction which took him completely off guard. He had thought until today that perhaps she was the rare kind of person who never got angry. But then, he really knew nothing at all about her.

His connection with Mary as a female sibling had begun in Africa when he had announced to the Sisters of Charity nursing staff, that she was 'Mary Murphy,' his comatose younger sister. After his sister's condition had stabilized, Mary was transported to a larger facility which had a 'high risk' maternity ward. The good sisters were told that the baby boy Mary had delivered in the modern hospital hundreds of miles away from their jungle clinic had been adopted by a couple from South Africa, three months after Mary's unexpected arrival in the bush.

The Sisters were very pleased that she had miraculously recovered from her illness and had delivered a healthy baby boy. They had asked God for such a miracle with their Christian prayers and Bundu healing rituals.

***

Mary saw the look of surprise on Donald's face when she complained about having to leave the hotel because of a company emergency. She desperately wanted to find Liffey, but did not dare to let on as she was fearful that Donald meant to harm the girl. She could not imagine *why* he would want to do this, but she had witnessed first-hand the tantrum he threw last night after she was unable to find Liffey in the crowd. His face had been a mask of undisguised rage.

Mary had also noticed the artificial arm and thick eyeglasses Donald was wearing today when he came to tell her they were leaving. What was *that* about? She probably would not have given the odd disguise a second thought if she had taken her pills this morning. *Who* was she living with? If it was Halloween, nobody had invited her to the costume party.

She was now truly afraid of Donald Smith. If her theory about the pills was correct, and they really *were* downers, then she had to get away from her brother, if he even *was* her brother, as soon as possible. She would not run from him today because she feared for Liffey's safety. If they were checking out of the hotel right now, then he would not have access to her young friend. Mary would leave with Donald submissively and without further questions, for Liffey's sake.

***

Blood and diamonds. In the recurring dream Mary had at least every three days, people around her were *afraid* of something. A man with a big diamond ring. Sometimes the ring was dripping with blood. Were they afraid of Donald? *He* wore a large diamond ring.

Mary sensed she had to completely hide from Donald the new mental and physical energy she was already experiencing from cutting back on her pills. She would do her best to act sluggish and flat as usual, so he would not suspect she had stopped taking his drugs. "How *could* I have been so stupid? I believed everything he told me and trusted him against my better judgment for ten whole years, and heaven only *knows* for *what* purpose!"

CHAPTER TWENTY-TWO

While Attorney Rivers conferred with Sam, and made what seemed to Liffey to be a million phone calls, Liffey began to write down everything she was thinking. It was almost impossible to keep the wild thoughts flying around in her sludgy head in any kind of order anymore.

She made a list of her brain's contents on this 'no school,' Monday morning in Chicago, Illinois, at the Palmer House Hotel. She used the *third* person, like it was somebody else she was writing about.

Liffey concluded her thoughts with three short sentences: "Liffey Rivers now believes the diamond 'M' lady might really be her mother after all. Her mother was supposed to have died in a plane crash but might actually be alive and living with the Skunk Man. Therefore, Liffey Rivers' mother must be out of her mind and needs help immediately."

***

Robert Rivers had organized a full-scale sting to reel in Donald at 2:00 p.m. He tried not to think about the possibility that the diamond 'M' lady might not show up at the booth this afternoon with Donald. If he did not find an answer soon that would explain who the lady on the airplane was, he was very much afraid he would not be able to keep up a strong front for his daughter. It was like his heart was breaking for the second time at the thought of losing the wife he had already lost once, all over again.

CHAPTER TWENTY-THREE

At 1:45 p.m. Robert Rivers put his hastily assembled task force in place. The five doors leading into the International Diamond Exhibition were guarded by armed federal marshals.

Attorney Rivers had called Interpol and informed them that the McFleury trail was hot again and that his daughter had positively identified him in Chicago. He also contacted Louise in St. Louis, who told him they had never picked up a trail for the 'Skunk Man,' whoever he was, after he had disappeared from the hotel lobby in St. Louis. His woman friend, who had been apprehended at the airport, and had cooperated at first, ultimately refused to identify and testify against him. She said she feared for her life and did not want to enter a federal witness protection program. "She took a 15-year prison sentence, rather than testify against this guy," Louise Anderson said. "And of *course* I will help with Liffey again. I am only sorry that all this is not yet over and done with."

"McFleury," Robert Rivers told Louise, had vanished outside Belfast City several days ago. "UK operatives think that he fled to Scotland by private yacht, but I think they are wrong, Louise. He is right here in Chicago, and by some freak act of nature, he and Liffey have butted heads again. This time, I am not taking any chances. Please come as soon as you can. I will keep my staff detectives with Liffey until then."

***

As planned, Robert Rivers entered the exhibition hall at 1:58 p.m. and turned left. He felt like his heart was going to burst. He dared not hope that his wife would actually be standing at the blue diamonds booth.

She was not standing there.

There was only a small sign on an easel which said: 'The Smithfield Diamond Group.' The diamonds were gone. The display case contained only a few discarded blue lights and a handwritten note in block letters which said: 'Sorry! Family Emergency! See You Next Time!'

Forensic Interpol agents began to inspect the booth for the little markers that people leave behind them: hairs, fibers, fingerprints and even dirt from their shoes. Anything they turned up in Chicago would be compared with the forensic evidence that had already been collected in Ireland.

The International Diamond Exhibition committee informed the authorities that the Smithfield Diamond Company had registered with them under the name 'Anthony Antoine, DBA The Smithfield Diamond Company.' The company had a Miami P.O. Box and phone number.

Interpol's preliminary investigation revealed that there was no such company and no such address. The phone number reached a recording which said, "Please try your number again," over and over. The company's e-mail address bounced messages back to the sender as 'undeliverable.' It was as if there never had been a blue diamonds booth, and any trace of the diamond 'M' lady had been permanently erased.

Robert Rivers was not surprised. He was only very sad that the mystery of the diamond 'M' lady remained unsolved and now he would have to tell Liffey who was upstairs anxiously waiting for the outcome. The only good news was that Interpol had new leads to follow and Liffey could get back to some kind of normal life again, "Whatever that is when it comes to Liffey Rivers," he thought, exhausted.

CHAPTER TWENTY-FOUR

Donald Smith sipped an orange juice as the plane began a sharp climb, arching over Lake Michigan. Chicago had gone well in spite of the fact that he had crossed paths again with the Irish dancer. His main objective at the diamond show had been accomplished. His operatives had moved the real diamond necklaces to their receivers and replaced them with imitation glass.

Some of the money he made on the Chicago transactions would end up in the hands of west coast African revolutionaries. They would use it to buy ammunition to continue blowing each other up. He didn't care what they did, so long as he got his cut, and the flow of diamonds kept streaming toward him. He thought it was about time to get back to Africa to make sure that his rebel-seized diamond mines were running at their optimum potential. He smiled to himself. "Maybe next time, the Sisters of Charity will have another sick 'sister' for me in their hospital. I think I have had enough of the one sitting next to me."

***

Mary Murphy pretended to be napping while she looked down at Chicago's vanishing skyline through the slits of her eyes. It had been seven hours since she took the half dose of today's morning pills and she was shaky and anxious. She sipped her bottled water and took another half dose of the afternoon pills.

The plane left Lake Michigan far below and began its direct path to Texas. Mary Murphy could not stop thinking about the clue she had left behind for Liffey. It was one chance in a million that Liffey would actually *find* it but she had to try *something*. She could not rely on fate to cross their paths again and she was desperate to warn Liffey about Donald's inexplicable when she had been unable to find her last night. She did not know why Liffey had disappeared and had not come back to the booth looking for her, but she suspected it had something to do with her brother.

On the large 'Group Messages' board in the hotel lobby, Mary had written:

Irish dancers: Please check in with Diamond M at Yahoo after check out.

Mary used a Yahoo e-mail address which her brother knew nothing about. She prayed that Liffey would see the Diamond M message. What were the odds that Liffey would figure it out even if she *did* see it? She counted on Liffey's fascination with her necklace. Liffey had inspected it two years ago in Texas like it was one of the Crown Jewels. *If* Liffey did see this message, Mary was fairly *certain* she would know it was from her. But would Liffey act on it? She wished she could have been more precise, but the hotel might have erased the message if it had not been addressed to a group. It was the only thing she could think of and she was astounded she had even had the idea in the first place. She could count all the ideas she had had in the past ten years on one hand.

CHAPTER TWENTY-FIVE

The drive back to Wisconsin seemed to take forever. Sam drove and Robert Rivers sat next to him in the front passenger seat. Liffey Rivers and Margaret, the other staff investigator her father had recruited, rode together in silence in the back seat.

All the way back to Wisconsin, Liffey thought about telling her father about the message board in the hotel lobby and the hint that it was from the diamond 'M' lady. Liffey did not tell him because she did not think he would be able to handle it. "After all," thought Liffey, "he had *hoped* that he might be reunited with my mother today after all these years."

Liffey had been walking right by the group message board in the hotel lobby when a baby girl in a stroller dropped a bottle of apple juice. It rolled across the carpeted floor. Liffey ran over to pick up the bottle for the screaming baby. As she stood back up, she could not *believe* what she was reading on a message board no more than six inches from her face! Liffey *knew* the message was meant for her. She would try experimenting with e-mail addresses as soon as she got back to her computer. If it *was* her mother, nothing could keep them apart any longer. Liffey would make sure of that.

***

The driver of the Olds 88 following the Rivers' automobile called himself 'Kenneth.' His motto was, "I 'KEN' do the job!"

He was careful to keep three car lengths between himself and his target.

Kenneth would bide his time and wait until it was precisely the right moment. Then he would earn his paycheck. So what if it took him several days? He had never been to this southern Wisconsin lake town which was only a few hours drive from Chicago. Maybe he could find a good restaurant and relax at one of the famous resorts he had seen advertised in the travel section of the Chicago Tribune. Maybe he would find a used book store and pick up a murder mystery. He had not read a good one in months.

It was obvious to Kenneth that the woman in the backseat next to the girl was a pro. He could see her watching all the angles behind her with small, directional mirrors. The driver of the car looked in his rear view mirror every thirty seconds. Like clockwork.

Kenneth pulled back a bit more so he would not be detected. There was no hurry. 'Operation Snow White' was in place. So was the poison for the apple.

CHAPTER TWENTY-SIX

When Liffey opened her eyes, they were approaching one of her Wisconsin nightmares: An *enormous* plastic elephant, a hideous clown and a life-size plastic giraffe. She closed her eyes again. She was almost home.

Liffey could *not* understand why this town, where she was *forced* to live, did not just 'get over' the past. Her father had told her that long ago, there were lots of circuses that 'wintered' here during the long months of snow and ice. What did 'wintered' mean anyway? "Those poor abused animals. I'm sure they just loved freezing to death in wooden barns until spring," Liffey thought. "Why would a circus hang around in a place where it snowed all winter anyway? Why not go 'winter' someplace warm?" Liffey was thankful that her father was not very interested in circus history because she never had to listen to circus history lectures. His specialty was Irish history and she had always been spared from his Irish lectures, unless it was St. Patrick's Day, or, as she now knew all too well, they were actually *in* Ireland.

She winced when Sam floored the gas pedal and they practically flew by the statue of the creepy clown. Her father must have told Sam about the clown thing. When Liffey was little, she used to cover her eyes when they drove by this clown. Liffey would scream and cry if her father forgot and took the main brick road through town and they had to drive by the clown statue, so Robert Rivers rarely took this route.

The creepy clown stood in a little park in the middle of the road like a menacing sentinel, just waiting for children to pass by. Clowns were *not* funny to Liffey. They were sinister and dangerous. Liffey had *always* hated clowns.

Her father had discovered how much she hated them one day when she was five years old. To help his daughter overcome her fear of the clown statue in the park, he took Liffey to the town's annual clown parade where clowns from all over the country assembled each year. The clowns would hang around together for several days before the parade, taking clown classes. After they had learned how to be funnier, they would march in a parade along the main street, honking horns and blowing loud whistles and waving frantically at everybody.

They often threw candy or interacted with the children in the crowd and this proved to be the undoing of a clown called 'Mud Puddles.' Mr. Puddles worked the crowd like he needed its feedback to live. He blew a loud whistle and wore a drab brown clown suit.

The clown wore brown and white face paint and thought it was very funny to splash little children's feet with a secret water pump. The water pump not only squirted water. When it was squeezed, it activated a loud siren which Mud Puddles kept in a burlap sack he carried over his shoulders. Mud Puddles spotted little Liffey Rivers standing along the curb with her father. She covered her tiny ears when the clown activated the siren which meant that the water pump would be squirting at someone's feet any second.

That someone turned out to be Liffey Rivers who watched in horror as Mud Puddles came at her grinning and spraying her shiny pink shoes with big squirts of water. The idea was to make a puddle underneath her feet. Instead of grabbing on nervously to her parent, and giggling like the other children in the crowd, Liffey charged Mud Puddles and repeatedly kicked the clown on his kneecaps and shins screaming *"Get out of here you monster!"* over and over. Mud Puddles lost his balance and hit the pavement.

Robert Rivers quickly removed the hysterical Liffey before she went at Mr. Puddles again on the ground. He carried her away from the parade route, kicking and screaming. Mud Puddles was assisted to his feet by paramedics, who were normally there to assist people who might become ill from heat exhaustion, not clowns who had been downed by five-year-old girls.

***

Liffey did not think that her father, the 'wanna be' shrink, had diagnosed her correctly regarding her 'condition.' He said she had 'coulrophobia.' "That's what it is called if you are afraid of clowns and want to run and hide when you see one," Robert Rivers had explained.

Liffey did not know why, if you just did not *like* clowns, or just did not want them *around you*, it had to be called a 'condition.'

Mustering up every bit of self control she could, Liffey forced herself to keep her coulrophobic mouth closed now and not tell her father about the message on the board in the hotel lobby. Deep down inside, she knew she *should* tell him. It was obviously the right thing to do. She just did not want him to flip out again. Liffey needed to get home and back on her computer to try out diamond 'M' addresses until she found the one which might lead her to Maeve McDermott.

Liffey had known from the start that something was a little bit 'off' about the diamond 'M' lady. She had seemed very hesitant and unsure about everything. "Everything except chili," Liffey thought, smiling. It was like she was *afraid* to say anything because she might say something wrong. Kind of like Liffey felt in math class if her teacher asked her for the answer to a problem. But by far Liffey's biggest concern at the moment was the fact that her mother, if it *was* her mother, apparently thought that the Skunk Man was her *brother* and obviously had no idea that Liffey might be her daughter.

Liffey *had* to figure out the e-mail address and warn her about how dangerous her 'brother' was. "She is not *safe* with that man," Liffey thought, remembering her terrifying ordeal in the stairwell in St. Louis. "The diamond 'M' lady would probably be safer if she lived in a cage with a rattlesnake."

There was also the question, *if* the diamond 'M' lady really *was* her mother, where had she *been* for the past ten years?

CHAPTER TWENTY-SEVEN

Kenneth worried that the lady with the little mirrors might have become suspicious of him and alerted the driver when he observed the silver BMW suddenly accelerate on the red brick road as it approached a strange island of peculiar animal statues. He thought he had taken great care to remain far enough behind them so as not to be detected, but in case he was wrong, he quickly made a right turn at the next corner and passed the small town police department on his left. Their dispatcher would be getting an emergency call for assistance in the not too distant future. But by the time the call came in, it would already be over.

Kenneth found the BMW easily after making two more quick turns. When he established exactly where they lived, he would go for a hamburger and then find the shiniest apples in town.

The substance he would use to coat the fruit would immediately cause the body to go into shock and create an irregular heartbeat. Death usually occurred within three hours. The best part was that his future victim did not even need to bite into the Snow White apple. The lethal toxin would pass into her blood stream by the simple act of touching one of his apples. All he had to do was to toss it into the target's hands. She would catch it, decline to accept it, and say, "No thanks." Then she would hand the apple back to him but it would be too late. He would, of course, be wearing gloves. The autopsy would conclude that the young victim had died from a drug overdose. The kind of 'kitchen chemist' drugs kids buy from each other for recreational purposes until the party's over and someone is in a coma or dead. The local coroner was not likely to suspect foul play.

Kenneth thought this girl looked a bit young for the accidental drug overdose method, but he assumed Smith knew what he was doing and Kenneth knew that large numbers of young teens were ruining their lives with drugs at very early ages these days. "Losers," he thought disgustedly. "Throwing away their lives like that."

***

Liffey calculated that the diamond 'M' lady would still be en route to Seattle, or Miami, according to the diamond exhibition officials. Liffey was betting on Seattle because she knew the diamond 'M' lady had lived there two years ago. This meant that Liffey would have a few hours yet to solve the e-mail riddle before the 'M' lady reached home. "It would be so amazing to have a message already waiting from me when she checks her mail," Liffey daydreamed.

***

When Donald told Mary that they were staying in Houston and were not continuing on to Seattle, she tried very hard not to display any emotion one way or the other. "Fine," she answered. "Where *are* we going then?" she asked vacantly.

Donald *almost* believed her passive response was genuine. It seemed *almost* normal, only he was fairly certain that Mary was playacting now. He could tell by her speech patterns that she was not as drugged as she should be. It was obvious to Donald she must be fooling around with her medications. Her hands were trembling and she looked pale. "That must be why she had the migraine headache this morning," he thought. "She's withdrawing."

Donald also picked up a vibe that Mary seemed somewhat uncertain of him now and he knew what had triggered it: "That Irish dancer." He could not take any more chances with either his 'sister' or her little friend, Liffey, who seemed to be on a crusade to ruin his life. They were both dispensable and he was sick of them.

Maybe by now Liffey was already history. He decided right then and there that Mary too would be history, just as soon as the opportunity presented itself.

CHAPTER TWENTY-EIGHT

A wide, paved driveway led down to the Rivers' split-level, lake front house. The view overlooking the small marina was idyllic. A forest of purple and white lilac bushes waited to bloom again next spring in the terraced side garden. Maeve McDermott was an architect and had designed and supervised this dream house which provided weekend sanctuary to the busy couple from their hectic working lives in Chicago. After Liffey arrived, Maeve spent all of her time with their daughter in Wisconsin and Robert Rivers began his long years of commuting.

***

Lewis, the Rivers' professional house sitter, waved at them from the enclosed front porch and Max the Magnificent ran out to greet them with his little tail wagging furiously. Liffey scooped Max up and walked quickly into the house and directly into her room. She hugged the aging brown terrier and played the 'I *see* you' game with him until he began to hyperventilate and needed to recover in his little dog bed underneath Liffey's computer. Liffey switched on the PC and heard Max already snoring as it booted up.

***

It was obvious to Mary that she had not deceived Donald with her agreeable "Anything is fine with me, Donald," answer.

He had pretended not to notice that she was different now, even though her hands trembled and her face occasionally twitched. She probably should be in some kind of medical emergency clinic in a drug withdrawal unit. She knew it could be fatal withdrawing from some drugs but she had no idea what drugs she had been taking for the past ten years. Whatever they were, they had to be in the 'sedative' family. She was weaning herself carefully, like a baby from milk to solid foods. When the pills were gone, she would be free of them forever and hopefully be her old self again, whoever that might be.

Now, however, she was not sure she *had* a week. She saw Donald's face when he had looked at Liffey in the crowd. He did not reveal that rage now, sitting next to her, but she could feel the anger in him heating up, and she was frightened. Surely he could see that she was in a weakened physical condition and very vulnerable? "I will *not* go anywhere alone with this man," she thought, feeling her self-survival instinct rising up from what felt like the bottom of an abandoned well. The 'defogger' was switched on in her head. She might be trembling and vulnerable, but she was no longer a robot. She was becoming a person again.

***

Liffey tried six Yahoo e-mail addresses with different combinations of the words 'diamond,' 'Irish,' 'dancer,' and 'lady,' with the letter 'M.' Five of the messages bounced right back as undeliverable. One of them did not come back! Liffey's message to the diamond 'M' lady was simple: "*Here I am! I saw your message in the hotel lobby! I can't wait to hear from you so we can talk! I hope this is the right address? Love—Liffey*"

Liffey hoped it would not be long until she had a reply. The message was either a bull's eye target hit or directed to the wrong person altogether in which case she would have to start all over again and perhaps never be successful. Liffey crossed her fingers, said a prayer and e-mailed Sinead in Ireland with a partial account of the past twenty-four hours.

"Sinead, you will NEVER believe this..."

***

"Must be nice to have money," Kenneth thought, cruising by the long, paved driveway the BMW had turned into. He would let them get settled while he went for a burger. Then he would check in at the cheap motel he saw a mile or so back. The produce section of a local supermarket would be next on his agenda. This summer had been hotter than usual which meant that shiny, fresh apples should be easy enough to find in early September. He wanted *the* apple to be irresistible.

Like the one Eve chose in the Garden of Eden.

CHAPTER TWENTY-NINE

Liffey thought that if she meditated next to her computer hard enough and long enough, she could *make* things happen. After all, the diamond 'M' lady *had* surfaced after she did the Zen exercises in the car on the way to the Palmer House Hotel.

Liffey also said a few 'Our Fathers.' She wanted to cover all the prayer bases and regretted that she did not know more about prayer traditions throughout the world. She was Catholic and usually went to Mass on Sundays if she could get her father out of bed. She always said special night prayers and had even read the Bible backwards once.

She drew the line at sacrificing goats, though. She had recently read about an airline that was having technical difficulties. The mechanics became more and more frustrated so they decided to sacrifice two goats on an airport runway to get their deity's attention. "That was totally bizarre. Those poor little goats," Liffey thought. "Like there could be a god who demanded that goats be sacrificed before an airplane could be fixed."

Liffey looked down at little Max in his dog bed and said, "You'd better behave, Mr. Dog, or I might have to sacrifice you to the computer gods!" Max did not seem to care and flipped over on his back with his paws extended upward like he was already dead or something. It was nice to be back with Max again.

***

Houston was hot and the humidity, suffocating. Mary was dripping with sweat. It felt like she was waiting for Donald in a sauna bath. She was glad he had volunteered to get the luggage because she doubted she had the strength at this point to carry her own bags. Donald hailed a cab before he arrived at Mary's waiting post and directed it to head for the northern suburbs. He asked the cab to pull into The Last Stop Motel, a dingy one storey concrete building, about a mile from the busy Houston airport.

"This is the kind of dump where people turn up dead after they have been missing for a month," Mary thought fearfully, making certain she signed in herself at the registration desk for her adjoining room. She wanted to make sure that there was a written record of her having stayed at this seedy place. She even complimented the greasy desk clerk's gold chain necklace so he would remember her. She could see the displeasure on Donald's face. He knew very well she was leaving bread crumbs behind like Hansel in case someone might be interested in following her trail. "But who would that be?" Donald sneered. "No one cares if she is living or dead."

It had seemed logical at first to be landing in Houston, since Donald had told her that they would be changing planes there. They had *not* changed planes, however, and there was no apparent reason to be staying in this tacky motel now. Mary feared the worst. She was careful not to display too much curiosity about her surroundings or Donald might become suspicious. She would have to sleep with both eyes open from now on and plot her escape. She sensed that the time had come when life with 'brother' was coming to an end. She was thankful that she was no longer completely under the influence of the pills. Now at least she would be able to fight back.

***

The first thing she needed to do was to get to a computer and see if Liffey had responded to the message she had left for her in the Palmer House lobby. She *had* to warn Liffey about Donald. It was a long shot, but somehow she had faith that Liffey would figure out the e-mail puzzle. *If* she had even seen her message to begin with! Mary knew that the odds were stacked against her.

Mary opened the heavy metal scuff-marked door to her room and placed her laptop and small suitcase on a grimy table. She was delighted to discover that there was an in-room modem link that looked like it was separate from the phone line. She could set up her laptop and log on immediately before Donald returned with the fast food he went out to find. It was perfect timing.

Mary went straight to her e-mail. There was one unread 'In' message. If this was some kind of moronic spam, she would break down and cry and probably throw things.

It was not spam. The sender was *Liffey!* Mary sighed with relief and hurriedly began to type a reply with her unsteady hands.

***

Liffey knew that *if* she heard back from the diamond 'M' lady, it was important to make arrangements to get together as soon as possible. "She needs to know that the Skunk Man is *not* her brother. He's a psychopath! And I can't just tell her in an e-mail that she is probably my *mother!* She might flip out and disappear again forever. I will have to show her the videotape and see if that jogs her memory."

***

Mary's answer to Liffey expressed her biggest concern: *"Liffey, how great to hear from you! I just knew you would see my message and figure out how to find me! I know it was a peculiar way to contact you, but normally hotels won't let people post their private e-mail addresses in lobbies so I had to be creative! I am so sorry we did not meet up last night. I could not find you in the crowd.*

You may think this is crazy, but I believe you may be in danger. My brother reacted very strangely when he saw you in Chicago. I cannot imagine why, but he seemed enraged. Anyway, he wanted me to find out where you live. There is no logical reason I can think of as to why he would have displayed such an interest in you. So please be careful!

Donald is with me now in Houston, but he has people who work for him in the Chicago area. You need to tell your father about this and do whatever he tells you. You should probably have him e-mail or call me (my number is below) for more information. I am planning on getting a place of my own this week and will let you know where I end up. Maybe then we can arrange to see each other again when it is convenient for you? If you have an Irish dance competition near me, I could come and watch you dance???

Please let me hear from you right away so I know you are safe. Love, Mary."

Message sent.

***

Liffey was ecstatic reading the reply to her message. She had correctly guessed the diamond 'M' lady's e-mail address! "She thinks the 'M' is for Mary," Liffey realized. Now they could plan a meeting and Liffey would find out once and for all if this mysterious woman was really her mother. Liffey knew her father would have to be involved at some point because only he could do a completely reliable identification. Liffey hesitated to do this right now because Robert Rivers seemed physically ill ever since he had gone looking for the diamond 'M' lady earlier today. Liffey could tell he was hurting a lot. Besides, she was certain she would be able to handle everything herself. The only significant problem Liffey could think of would be slipping away from her bodyguards. Liffey had to get to the 'M' lady as quickly as possible to warn her about the Skunk Man, whether she *was* or was *not* her mother.

CHAPTER THIRTY

Donald quietly slipped back into his motel room with two large bags containing fried chicken dinners with sides of mashed potatoes and gravy. The door adjoining Mary's room was slightly ajar and he could hear her typing quickly on her laptop. This prompted him to take the three emergency pills from his coat pocket and mix them into Mary's mashed potatoes. Mary must be starving by now since he had insisted they check out of the hotel before she was able to eat breakfast. And 'lunch' had consisted of ten tiny pretzels on the plane. "Mary," he called out to her, "come and get your chicken. I twisted my ankle in a pothole walking across the parking lot."

Mary hesitated but the delicious aroma of the chicken dinner lured her to the door. She looked into Donald's room and saw that he was lying on his bed with a TV clicker in one hand and a chicken leg in the other. Surely she could safely eat a dinner he had *just* brought in from an outside fast food restaurant? He gestured to her that her food was on the scratched-up dresser next to his bed. Mary could easily reach it without stepping into Donald's room. She quickly picked up the food bag, and closed the door without mentioning his ankle.

"You're very welcome!" Donald shouted through the door impatiently.

"Thanks a lot for the food. Hope your ankle is better soon," Mary replied in a monotone voice.

Mary knew better. She had intended not to eat or drink anything Donald would put in front of her ever again but she was so very, very hungry and after all, she *had just* heard Donald return with this food. She really was not even absolutely certain that he had noticed the change in her behavior. He had not mentioned her trembling hands or jitteriness. He would not make his move this soon anyway. If he wanted her out of the way, he would probably wait until she was asleep and arrange an 'accident,' like setting fire to her room. She could safely eat this food. She *had* to eat because she felt faint. Mary picked up the plastic spoon and greedily dug into the tasty mashed potatoes with gravy on the side.

***

Donald glanced over at his sleeping sister as he deleted Mary's first message to Liffey which was stored in her 'Sent' folder. Then he drafted another message *to* Liffey *from* his comatose sister. He was fairly certain the interfering dancer would take the bait.

"Liffey! I have to see you asap. You need to be very careful now as I am positive Donald, intends to harm you. Is there any way we can meet in Ireland and plan things? I know it sounds crazy, because in my first message I said I was going to look for a place to live and then hopefully connect with you. Now I have an overwhelming feeling that you must get out of the country immediately. Let's do something really crazy like meeting on top of a mountain! We could meet up on top of Knocknarea in Sligo? Yes, let's do Knocknarea. I have heard it is really amazing up there. Let's both be up there the day after tomorrow—Wednesday, at 4:00 p.m. We better not meet at the airport as Donald might follow me. So let's go separately. I will fly out of Houston tomorrow to Atlanta and then on to Shannon airport. Then I will rent a car and drive to Sligo. You fly to Dublin. When

you get to Dublin, take the airport shuttle to the bus station. It is only a few blocks from there to Connelly Station, where you can catch the train to Sligo. Then, when you get to Sligo, grab a cab. It's a short trip to Strandhill. About fifteen minutes. Make sure you tell the driver to take you to the car park next to the path up the mountain. It takes about an hour to climb up from there. I will be waiting for you! I can't wait to see you! This is very exciting! Love-Mary.

    P.S. We can find some Irish dancers too!"

Message sent.

***

Mary woke up with another terrible headache. The last thing she remembered was shoveling warm mashed potatoes into her mouth. She could see its empty red and white container to the left of the laptop as she stood up unsteadily and slowly made her way over to the computer. She sat down on the uncomfortable chair in front of the machine and turned it on, even though her head felt like it was splitting apart. She was delighted to see there was a reply from Liffey: *"Yes, I can get to Sligo and will meet you on top of Knocknarea by Queen Maeve's grave. You are right, I should get out of here if Donald is looking for me. I think I know why he might be after me. I will tell you when I see you. But right now we need to meet to talk about these things where we will both be safe. Ireland is a great idea. I will be on the mountain the day after tomorrow (Wednesday) at 4:00 p.m. Make sure you bring a raincoat!!! Love-Liffey. P.S. I will tell my dad all about everything and he will probably come with me so don't worry about anything. Just be there! Love-Liffey"*

Mary stared at the computer dumbfounded. Had she had a blackout? Liffey had 'replied' to a message she could not even *remember sending!* And in the 'Sent' folder, there was no record of the original message she thought she *had* sent to

Liffey. Instead, there *was* a long message suggesting that Liffey meet her in Ireland! "I told her *that?*" Mary was completely bewildered. "What is Knocknarea?" Had she researched Ireland online before dispatching the message? *How* did she give Liffey directions for getting to a place she knew nothing about? Had she spent time in Ireland prior to her amnesia? Was she flipping back and forth between the present and her forgotten past? But why in the world would she suggest a child meet her out of the country? "Have I completely lost my *mind?*"

***

Donald clicked off the boring movie with the high-speed chases. He wondered if Mary had come out of her stupor yet and read the predictable reply to the second message he had sent the little nuisance in Mary's name. He had been 100% positive that the wig brain was going to jump at the chance to interfere in his life again.

He had called the 'Snow White' hit off several hours ago. This was a much more efficient plan. He would rid himself of both of them at the same time. He probably would miss Mary sometimes, as she had proven to be very useful to him over the years. But she had changed. There was no doubt in his mind that things between them were different now, and he did not care enough about her to figure out what it was. As for the Irish dancer, she had meddled in his life for the *last* time. Donald could not understand why it was so important to Mary to link up again with a brat she had only met once, two years ago.

***

Kenneth received a one line text from Donald: *Snow White will not bite the apple.* Kenneth was pleased that he could enjoy his burger now without having to think about bodyguards and ending a young life. He would be paid either way and it was always much more pleasant if he did not have to *earn* his paycheck.

***

Liffey tried to distract herself from this incredible turn of events by starting to read *War and Peace* again. Her reading teacher said last year, that not one student in any of the reading classes she had taught over the past fifteen years had ever finished this book and received the maximum number of points you could earn in the reading challenge program. Liffey was determined to be the first student ever to finish *War and Peace* and then take the test to prove she had actually read it and not just watched the movie or something. After she read the book, she would nail her hornpipe steps. She was not sure why these two things were connected, but somehow she knew that they were. First, read *War and Peace*. Then, master the dreaded hornpipe.

CHAPTER THIRTY-ONE

As usual, *War and Peace* put Liffey to sleep in five minutes. Twenty minutes later, she woke up with a start. She lifted Max out of his little bed and rubbed noses with him. Max loved it when she did that. Then she tucked him under her left arm, and turned to the computer. She re-read the second message from the diamond 'M' lady. She could hardly believe it. Now the diamond 'M' lady wanted to meet her on top of the very mountain where Liffey had watched her mother on the videotape. This *had* to be fate! She knew the moon was trying to tell her something important was going to happen on Knocknarea!

***

Robert Rivers paced around the large oval living room with its yellow half moon couches and Liffey's favorite oak rocking chair while he explained the situation to Louise Anderson. Margaret and Sam had gone back to Chicago after the St. Louis detective had arrived. It was almost dark and the world outside the large picture window seemed menacing and dangerous. The only ripples on the placid lake were created by a mother duck and her eight ducklings. A lake could hide a body. The thick woods surrounding the house could easily conceal someone who was waiting for a chance to gain entry and harm his daughter. Liffey had been in her bedroom since they returned. "She's probably sleeping," Louise said comfortingly.

"Liffey's a tough little girl, Robert, she can handle this." "I hope you're right, Louise. I have a bad feeling this time."

***

Mary read the e-mail again she must have sent to Liffey and Liffey's reply agreeing that they would meet on Wednesday on top of a mountain called Knocknarea.

"My withdrawal must be very serious," she thought. "I cannot even remember sending the second message. And where is my *first* message? I am *sure* I sent it. Why in the world would I suggest meeting her on top of a mountain?"

On a *mountain?* Was *this* the same dream she had on the plane to Chicago? Had she *completely* flipped out earlier and sent *another* e-mail to Liffey while she had been *dreaming again?* The mountain top dream with the little girl running to her had been every bit as disturbing as the recurring dream she was always having about being so sick and hot and the far away crying baby.

Was *Liffey* the little girl in the mountain dream, and was she also the crying baby in the other dream as well? Should she e-mail yet *another* message and ask Liffey to please disregard all of her messages because she was apparently crazy?

Liffey had agreed to meet her on top of a mountain in County Sligo in Ireland. A place called Knocknarea. Mary clicked on her laptop's 'history.' It revealed she had apparently been online surfing Irish websites when she thought she had been asleep. Just like someone normal who was arranging a trip to Ireland!

In spite of deep reservations, something within her told her that she should let matters stay as they were. Donald was a heavy sleeper. She would leave at 6:00 a.m. and catch any airline's flight to Atlanta she could get. She would then head to Ireland and let fate take its course. She would not be at all surprised if she woke up in an insane asylum.

***

"Louise!" Liffey exclaimed with genuine delight. "When did *you* get here? How long are you *staying?*" While she was very happy to see Louise again, she hated the thought of having to ditch her tomorrow like she had done once before in St. Louis. Liffey *had* to get to Chicago tomorrow by 4:00 p.m. so she could check in for her Dublin flight. Everything was at stake. She might lose the diamond 'M' lady forever if she did not make it to the mountain Wednesday afternoon. Or, she might disappear again for another ten years and Liffey would be totally grown up if they ever met again. Liffey recalled the overpowering urge she had to run back *up* Knocknarea last Saturday immediately *after* she and her father had struggled in the fog to get *down* the mountain. Liffey was *positive* the moon had been telling her that something amazing was going to happen on the summit of Knocknarea. This was what she was *supposed* to do. Liffey knew it. It was her destiny. The beams of moonlight had pointed to the place where the life of Liffey Rivers was going to be altered forever when she would be reunited with her mother!

***

Donald was pretty sure both Mary and the wig-girl would walk right into his trap. He made his reservation to Dublin by way of Boston. He did not want to risk a chance meeting with either of them.

The rendezvous would be Wednesday afternoon on top of Knocknarea. He had never even noticed the towering mountain in Sligo until he was driving toward Sligo Town on his way to

Northern Ireland after the Beltra Feis fiasco. He noticed the bump on top of the mountain, and asked a Texaco petrol cashier what it was. She told him that the bump was the grave marker of the ancient Queen Maeve of Connaught. Donald had no idea what Connaught was and was not the least bit interested in finding out. Just to make conversation with the cashier, he had asked a typical tourist question. "How do you get up that mountain? I will have to climb it the next time I get back here."

Donald knew he would have to create an entirely new look for his return trip to Ireland tomorrow and he was more than prepared. He had several identities and passports he had never used. Tomorrow he would be 'Frank Fitzgerald,' a balding, middle-aged man, with a pronounced overbite and green eyes. "What did people do before tinted contact lenses and affordable dentures?" he thought. "And good hair dyes?"

The 'next time' back to Ireland had certainly come sooner than expected. The really handy bit of information he had received at the petrol pump in Sligo was that, while most people walked up Knocknarea from the parking lot half-way up the mountain on the south side, others rode up the mountain on *horseback* from the east. There were riding stables at the base of Knocknarea and he just happened to be an expert horseman. This was going to be fun. He had read once in a magazine that the British aristocracy called hunting animals 'blood sport.' That phrase described his intentions perfectly.

***

Louise's arrival definitely complicated things for Liffey. Louise would keep a close eye on her because she knew Liffey could be slippery. Liffey would have to plan her escape to Ireland tomorrow very carefully. Every tiny detail needed to be mapped out tonight.

Liffey printed the ticket she purchased online using her own savings account. Her father did not know her password, so he would not be able to find the airline ticket withdrawal. She had her passport. She had about one hundred euro left for the upcoming train and cab fares in Ireland this Wednesday and she had enough American money to pay the local taxicab driver tomorrow who would pick her up and take her to the airport shuttle bus. She printed and then filled out the forms giving permission to herself to travel alone. Finally, she sneaked into her father's bedroom while he was talking with Louise and removed the videotape from his carry-on bag.

The *biggest* problem would be escaping from Louise tomorrow. Louise was a good detective. She would know how to look on Liffey's computer for clues as to where she might have gone. Liffey would have to put her on false trails and file the diamond 'M' lady's e-mail and her own mail into secret folders.

The ultimate challenge would be how to divert Louise and her father long enough to have the reunion on the mountain top with Mary. She did *not* want to alarm her poor father and did not want Louise to hate her for doing this ditching thing again. She had told Mary she would at least tell her father, and maybe even bring him along with her, but ultimately decided Robert Rivers was not up for another possible letdown.

Of course there was also the problem of having to show up at school tomorrow with her own private *bodyguard* which would be so completely humiliating, Liffey refused to think about it now. She would have to get *out* of the school without Louise discovering her absence for as long as possible.

Liffey knew that no one, including Louise, would *ever* suspect she was off to Ireland again tomorrow. Why would they? There was no link to Ireland with the diamond 'M' lady and as far as her father knew, the diamond 'M' lady was with her 'brother' on the way to Miami. He did not even know about the message riddle and how Liffey had solved it and planned to meet with Mary on a mountain in Ireland. How on earth could anyone ever imagine such a scenario?

Liffey had another little twinge of conscience telling her that this was *not* the right thing to do. She *really* should tell her father and they should *both* go Ireland and climb up Knocknarea again to meet with the diamond 'M' lady.

"I am *not* going to risk breaking daddy's heart. He's had enough misery. Besides, what could *possibly* be dangerous about climbing up Knocknarea again?"

So it was settled. Liffey would do this alone.

CHAPTER THIRTY-TWO

There was no time to sleep tonight even though Liffey knew she was already getting drowsy. She could sleep on the plane tomorrow night on her way back to Ireland. They were six hours ahead over there. She would leave Chicago at 6:00 p.m. when it would already be midnight in Ireland. She would arrive in Dublin when it would still be the middle of the night in Chicago. She *had* to sleep on the plane tomorrow.

Right now she needed to plan every move she would make in the next twenty-four hours. On the other hand, she *could* sleep a few hours tonight after she completed her plans...

***

The obnoxious 'Chicken Dance' alarm sounded, jolting Liffey into a happy state of wakefulness because today was *the* day! Max growled from the foot of the bed. Max *hated* the Chicken Dance song. Liffey switched it off and Max turned over with a loud gurgling exhale. She hoped he was not slobbering on her quilt again.

Liffey had been able to cram everything she would need for her trip into her school backpack. Her father would have already left for his office commute to Chicago. Liffey's first task this morning was to act like it was an ordinary day. She could not let on how anxious she was during breakfast.

"Good morning, Liffey!" Louise said with a positive thinking kind of inflection. "Hey, same to you, Louise," Liffey answered, rubbing her eyes, pretending to be groggy. "Ready to get back to school?" "Never," Liffey replied. Louise smiled. So far, so good.

"Liffey, I have already spoken with the Assistant Principal this morning and he has assured me we can keep this bodyguard matter confidential," Louise said pouring Cheerios into a large bowl for Liffey. "I will spend today touring the school like a new employee. Tomorrow, I will actually *be* in the office. I can see from in there if anything or anyone unusual is approaching the school. Your father made a generous donation to the school building fund to make everyone cheerful about this imposition. He also assured them that it would only be a temporary situation," Louise finished.

"That's for sure," thought Liffey, eating one dry cheerio at a time for good luck, and mentally going over today's escape plan.

***

It took Louise five minutes to inspect the Rivers' property prior to their departure for what Louise anticipated would be a day of ordinary surveillance at the local middle school. On the way, to keep Louise from being suspicious, Liffey tried to be chatty and even acted excited about her first day back to school, saying things like, "I wonder if Nicole Woods still has her red highlights?" Liffey did not even know anyone named Nicole Woods.

When they arrived at the school parking lot, Louise parked the car right in front of the school entrance doors instead of parking in the lot with all the other cars. "Too easy to hide between cars in a parking lot," she told Liffey who was already beginning to cringe. She gestured for Liffey to follow her and opened the passenger car door like some kind of chauffeur.

Liffey winced when she noticed that other students, who were arriving late like she was, were openly staring at her. "I'm so *out* of here in three hours anyway. I guess I can last until then and play bodyguard with Louise," Liffey told herself.

For once, Liffey did not have to crawl past the office Dutch door while Godzilla was broadcasting his pathetic joke of the day. She gave a little parade wave to the secretaries and not one of them charged at her with a detention. Liffey enjoyed this new feeling of not being in trouble with the office because she was tardy.

Her new homeroom teacher was obviously not aware that Liffey had *carte blanche* today to be late because she slammed the door right in Liffey's face as she was going in. "Back to prison life," Liffey thought, as she knocked on the door for permission to enter and the detention she was sure to receive before she even started this semester.

***

At precisely 11:30 a.m., the lunch bell rang. Liffey Rivers went to her locker and took out her stuffed backpack. The halls were crowded with hungry students stampeding towards the cafeteria. Liffey joined them but then abruptly turned right and ran down a deserted hallway. Then she smashed the protective seal surrounding Hall B's fire alarm and pulled the lever. The screeching fire alarm immediately caused the sort of pandemonium Liffey had hoped it would. She deftly unlocked the west wing 'Fire Exit' door, carefully jamming the screwdriver she had removed from her father's tool box into the outside door lock to prevent the students who were supposed to exit from this door from leaving this way.

"It's a good thing I'm an Irish dancer in great shape," Liffey thought, sprinting towards her old primary school driveway fifty yards away. When she had almost reached her destination, she saw an old red Ford Escort simultaneously pulling into the circular drive. It had a stick-on 'Taxi' sign in the rear window. Everything depended on her getting into that taxi and off school property before her absence was detected by Louise. She was fairly confident that the school office personnel would not be able to efficiently manage the chaos created by the strident fire alarm siren on only the second day of classes. The office would, of course, *know* it was not a practice drill and Liffey was certain Godzilla would be on the intercom right now saying something to make things worse like, "This is *not* a drill!" That would make everybody totally panic and it could be a half hour or so before things calmed down enough for Louise, or one of the roll-taking teachers, to realize someone named Liffey Rivers was not standing in her assigned spot.

***

Liffey jumped quickly into the cab and surveyed the soccer fields behind her. There was no one following her. The hall door jam had apparently held and all of the action was happening in front of the school where the students would be lining up into pre-arranged fire drill lines at a safe distance from the school.

She could hear fire trucks screaming in the distance and cheerfully thanked the cab driver for being on time. "I am going to South Beloit for the O'Hare shuttle bus, but I suppose they told you that." "Yep," the cab driver replied, gunning the cab like it was some kind of emergency vehicle and exiting the primary school grounds in seconds. "They told me."

Liffey tried not to dwell on how many fire alarm melodramas she had been part of recently. There was the London art gallery exodus and the Beltra Hall evacuation and now *this*! Liffey knew it was totally wrong to be leaving this way and that it was probably some kind of a serious crime as well to set off a fake fire alarm, but she could not think of any other way to escape. It really *was* a matter of life and death for the diamond 'M' lady. Liffey *had* to meet her on the mountain tomorrow and that meant she *had* to do desperate things! Liffey was counting on her father's forgiveness when she came back from Ireland with his *wife*. She *hated* to temporarily cause what she knew would be *extreme* worry on his part, but it would all be over tomorrow when she would call him from Knocknarea and let him talk with her mother!

CHAPTER THIRTY-THREE

Robert Rivers cancelled his afternoon meetings and raced back to Wisconsin. *This* time, Liffey had gone *too* far! *This* time, he would punish her severely! How *dare* she spring a fire alarm at school and then just disappear? *What* was she thinking?

***

Firemen searched the school building and assured Louise that there was no one hiding inside. *Why* was Liffey doing this? Although the police had not yet accused her, it seemed fairly obvious to Louise that Liffey was the one who triggered the fire alarm and then bolted. Robert Rivers had told her that Liffey was very reluctant to return to school, but *surely* Liffey knew that this was completely unacceptable behavior?

A disturbing thought crossed Louise's mind. What if Liffey had *not* engineered this event? What if she had been abducted somehow in the middle of all of the confusion? This thought chilled Louise's blood and she had to sit down, weak and dizzy, on the stairs leading into the gymnasium. "Have I screwed up? Had someone *else* triggered the fire alarm? Someone who was already lurking inside the school before Liffey and I even got here?"

Louise grabbed the banister and pulled herself up. She needed to find the Chief of Police and get an all-points bulletin out with Liffey's photo. Somehow, Louise did not think Liffey was capable of deliberately putting her father through this kind of terror. Liffey was flaky but not cruel.

On a hunch, Louise decided she would check Liffey's locker before she got the police actively involved. It was unlocked. Inside, scotch-taped to the door, was an envelope addressed to *"Louise and Daddy."* She tore it open and read: *"Please don't be too mad!! I HAD to do this!! I am totally safe and will call you tomorrow afternoon and explain everything. Love-Liffey. P.S. Daddy, you will be soooooooo happy tomorrow!"*

"I have to *think* like a 13-year-old," Louise thought. "What is Liffey *thinking*? Surely she knows that she is putting herself at risk doing this. And what does she think I am *doing* here anyway? Babysitting?"

***

Mary looked down at the Gulf of Mexico far below. *Why* had she told Liffey she would meet her on top of a mountain in Ireland tomorrow? She *was* withdrawing from her medications and had bouts of nausea and tremors pretty much constantly now, but was she also completely insane? That might explain why she had set up such a ridiculous spot for their meeting. Obviously her brain was malfunctioning. Also, she could not shake the feeling that Liffey was in immediate danger because of Donald. "I will call her father the second we meet up, just in case Liffey conveniently 'forgets' to bring him along with her. *What* kind of an adult am I? I should have called and verified with her parent that she had his consent. Maybe I should have gone to rehab before I took on the world again? My decision making skills are obviously pathetic."

***

'Special Agent' Frank Fitzgerald flashed his toothy smile at the ticket counter personnel and checked one bag through. In that bag was a gun with a valid permit to carry a weapon. "It helps to have connections in the right places," he thought, as he passed through airport security and headed towards his departure gate.

***

Liffey Rivers sighed with relief when it was at last time to board her flight to Dublin. "It won't be long now," she thought, with a contented sigh.

CHAPTER THIRTY-FOUR

The forensic computer specialists Louise had contacted after she was unable to find any hidden e-mails or secret folders on Liffey's computer, were not able to get to Wisconsin until 8:30 p.m. When they finally arrived, they immediately began to dissect the hard drive. "This will probably take several hours," they informed Robert Rivers and Louise. "We will work as quickly as possible, but this could take a good bit of time."

Time. Robert Rivers hoped that they *had* time as he made a fourth pot of coffee. The local police had put out an all-points bulletin in Wisconsin with Liffey's photo, and had been searching for her ever since the fire drill exit lists had revealed she was gone. Robert Rivers and Louise had each made their own rounds, questioning local restaurants and businesses. When Louise had called the local taxi cab company, thinking that Liffey was not old enough to drive a car and fairly certain she was not so naive or stupid enough to hitchhike, the answering service operator had said that both company cabs were in the garage for routine maintenance and had been all day.

What the cab company phone service did not know, was that one of its drivers had illegally used his own car earlier in the day to drive a young girl to the O'Hare Airport shuttle bus to make some extra cash. After he dropped her off at the bus stop in Illinois, he turned around and drove to his favorite fishing lake in the middle of nowhere. It was nice to get a day off once in awhile when the company cabs went in for maintenance. There were no televisions or radios or newspapers in his fishing cabin and the money he got from his young passenger today would pay for carryout food tonight and a new fishing license.

***

"If *only* Liffey had friends here, Louise. Then I could at least interview them and maybe construct some kind of theory as to what she is up to."

"First of all, you don't *interview* young teenage girls, Robert," Louise said diplomatically. "You *talk with* them and hope one of them says something useful."

Robert Rivers acknowledged this criticism graciously and said, "Sadly, there is not even one name that comes to mind. Not one. I am afraid that I have been very remiss in not doing something about Liffey's isolation here. She was so happy in Ireland with Sinead. I never saw her like that before. She just seemed to fit in naturally."

Louise, startled to hear a name at last, asked the logical question, "*Who* is Sinead, Robert, and *how* do we contact her?" "I don't have her mobile number. I suppose it's on Liffey's cell phone," Robert Rivers answered. "Do you know her *last* name?" Louise continued hopefully. "No. I don't," was his exasperated reply.

Louise groaned. It was going to be long night. In a few more hours, she would call County Sligo, Ireland, and try to find a list of dancers who had attended the Beltra Feis. Then she would contact all the Sineads who had danced at the competition last Saturday and hopefully locate Liffey's friend.

***

Liffey could see what had to be Iceland far below, like some kind of Middle Earth in an endless ocean of green water. It would not be long now before she would land in Ireland, and begin her new life with the mother she never dared to *imagine* could actually be out there somewhere. She tried not to get her hopes up because she knew that the diamond 'M' lady might *not* be her mother. But then, who else *could* she be? Her father had showed her that videotape and he *said* that the woman in it was Maeve McDermott, her dead mother. Liffey knew for a *fact* that the woman in the tape was alive. She had been with her two years ago on the flight from Pittsburgh to Seattle, and then *again* in Chicago. "This is going to be epic," Liffey thought happily, closing her eyes for a final snooze before landing.

***

"I think we've got something here, Attorney Rivers." It was 5:00 a.m. Wednesday morning. Robert Rivers walked over to the forensic computer technicians, trying not to get his hopes up. It had been an endless, frustrating night, following the false leads Liffey had carefully planted pointing towards Disneyworld, Disneyland, Sea World in San Diego and San Francisco. This morning, up until now, had been maddening. "We have a message here from a woman named Mary asking Liffey to meet her on top of a mountain called Knocknarea somewhere in Ireland tomorrow. That would be today."

Robert Rivers felt his heart stall. His daughter had fallen right into the hands of the very people he had feared all along were going to harm her. He numbly dialed the law firm's pilot on call and instructed her to file a flight plan and then ready the plane for an immediate flight to Ireland. They would have to land at Knock Airport in County Mayo, about 50 miles from Strandhill. He would need a helicopter to be waiting at Knock to take them to Knocknarea. It might come down to an air rescue if the local Gardai had not found Liffey before he arrived. "It is already 11:00 a.m. in Ireland," he thought dejectedly, as he dialed the Sligo Gardai Station to discuss the latest Liffey Rivers catastrophe. At least he had established some credibility with the Gardai when he had alerted them about the art thieves at Beltra last Saturday.

Last Saturday? Had it only been *four days* since this had all begun?

CHAPTER THIRTY-FIVE

Dublin's airport was low key compared to all the armed police and customs officials swarming around Chicago's O'Hare International Airport. Since Liffey only had her backpack, she went directly to passport control, and then right out of the airport past an empty customs desk.

The day was overcast and cool. She found a shuttle bus right outside the arrivals doors and jumped on just as it was pulling out. Her plane had been delayed in Chicago, but she still had plenty of time to make the 11:00 a.m. train to Sligo. It was a three hour trip from Dublin to the Sligo train station and then another twenty minutes by taxi to the mountain car park, but it was still quite possible that she would be able to get up Knocknarea by 4:00 p.m. "I climbed it last Saturday in forty-five minutes," she recalled.

Last *Saturday*? Had it only been *four days* since this had all begun?

"How could so much have happened in such a short time?" Liffey asked herself. With the time difference, it had barely been four days. She hoped her father was coping with her disappearance and not becoming even crazier. He might at this very moment be out riding around in another taxi cab. Anyway, it would only be another few hours until she would be able to call him with the wonderful news. "I *have* to call Aunt Jean about daddy," Liffey reminded herself.

***

Mary hired a driver to take her from Shannon Airport to Strandhill because she did not want to drive on the left hand side of the road while she was jet lagged *and* experiencing serious withdrawal symptoms. The bus connections were too complicated for her to sort out. She felt weak and breathless. "The way I feel, I may have to *crawl* up that mountain," she thought wearily. Maybe she and Liffey would actually *meet* on the climb up. As soon as they did meet, she would call Liffey's father and let him know about her concerns with Donald. She should have done that *before* she told Liffey to meet her in Ireland in that strange e-mail that she could not even *remember* sending.

"Liffey's father might have me arrested and I would not blame him one bit." Mary had absolutely *no idea* why she felt she *had* to do this! It was like a powerful magnetic force was pulling her in this direction. A force so strong it could not be resisted.

***

Just in case her father had been able to figure out where she was going and got all bent out of shape and tried to stop her, Liffey had taken a few precautions. After she boarded the train to Sligo, she immediately went into the toilet and put on the oversized fake prescription glasses she had used in London at the National Portrait Gallery.

True, the glasses had not worked there, but that was *only* because of that security guard who had started babbling at her in *real* Spanish after she spoke the only sentence she could actually get out of her mouth in Spanish. How could *she* have known he would be able to rattle off Spanish words like a machine gun? He had obviously detected she was not a native Spanish speaker and then alerted the police, who were roaming all over the gallery, to pick her up for questioning. "It was *not* because my *disguise* failed. It was because of my totally lame *Spanish*!"

Liffey decided it would be a good idea to look considerably older now than her thirteen years. She rummaged through her backpack and took out the cheap purse she bought outside the train station from a street vendor. She applied the dark pink lip gloss she brought along. She smiled. Her lips looked at *least* eighteen-years-old.

Next, she bobby pinned her hair up in strips and slipped on the short blond wig her Aunt Jean had given her for her thirteenth birthday so she could look like someone Aunt Jean loved but Liffey had never even heard of before.

Liffey tried to objectively review her completed disguise in the blurry mirror. She was confident that she looked nothing like the young American escapee whose picture might well be all over Ireland by now if her father had somehow figured things out.

She had purchased *The Irish Times* in the train station before boarding so she could pretend to be reading on the train. "Only adults read *The Irish Times*," she reasoned, as she applied the ruby stick-on earrings she came across inside a forgotten backpack compartment. Liffey did not have pierced ears and she was certain her father would have told the authorities to look for ears which were *not* pierced if he had filed a report. The fake ruby earrings definitely gave Liffey's ears a pierced look.

Liffey was confident now that she looked like another person altogether. She walked back out into what had become a very crowded coach and sat down next to an eccentric looking woman who was conversing loudly with herself. "The police are bound to focus on this poor creature and skip over me if they happen to be looking." She opened up *The Irish Times,* spread it out over her lap, and pretended to be asleep. Irish people were usually so polite it was highly unlikely anyone would try to wake up this sleeping university student. "And if they do, then I'm doomed and *totally* finished because my Irish accent is about as believable as the Lucky Charms Leprechaun," Liffey thought, resigned to whatever her fate would be.

CHAPTER THIRTY-SIX

Frank Fitzgerald reserved the sleek black horse for five hours. He paid in cash. After assuring the staff at the riding center that he was an experienced rider, he was given a map showing the path up Knocknarea through the pine forest on the east side of the mountain. "I prefer to ride alone," he said, watching a group of five riders trotting off with their guide to explore the nearby antiquities.

He deftly mounted his steed and was pleasantly surprised when the horse responded quickly to his commands. "His name is *El Diablo*," the groom told Mr. Fitzgerald as the horse neighed and stomped, anxious to leave the stables and begin the long trek. "How appropriate," Frank Fitzgerald observed. He kicked the stallion gently and moved out onto the trail.

***

Mary arrived at the Knocknarea car park at 1:00 p.m. It was empty. She was fairly certain that no one had followed her there. "Three hours should allow me enough time to get up the mountain by 4:00 o'clock," she thought.

"Are you sure you want me to be leaving you here now?" the hired driver inquired. "Yes, thanks very much," Mary answered, adjusting her backpack straps, as she sucked in big gulps of cool, moist sea air. "Liffey is bound to catch up with me on the way up, if she's not already there."

***

The train pulled into the Sligo Train Station at precisely 2:00 p.m. Liffey quickly scanned the crowd waiting to board the train on the platform. She saw no one who appeared to be police as she pressed the large green exit button by the door and stepped down on to the platform.

"Wonderful!" Liffey muttered, when she saw the human barricade of police officers in their neon yellow jackets blocking the only exit from the train station. There was no where to go but straight through them.

Liffey was not at all confident her disguise would work. She felt her chest tightening and reached for her asthma inhaler in her jacket pocket. If her father had told the police to look for an asthmatic, she was would be immediately detected and taken directly to the Sligo Gardai Station. She would never be able to explain to them that they *had* to let her go because the diamond 'M' lady was in danger because the man she *thought* was her brother was not *really* her brother, but an international criminal. If she also told them that the diamond 'M' lady called herself Mary, but was really Maeve, her missing mother, who was now up on Knocknarea waiting for her, they would probably take her straight to the local mental hospital. She *had* to get through this police line!

She thought of a line from a movie about the Irish patriot Michael Collins that her father had made her watch a million times. *"If you want to hide, act like no one is looking for you."* This seemed like good advice at the moment as well as her only option. She deliberately stepped right in front of the police line. They were all looking at her. She drew in two short blasts of medication from her inhaler. A garda approached her and her heart almost stopped beating.

This kind of strategy had *always* worked for Michael Collins in the movie! After what seemed like centuries, the garda spoke with obvious concern in his voice, "Are you all right, young lady?" She dared not answer him with her bogus Irish accent, so she nodded silently, like she was suffering greatly from this breathing condition, and smiled bravely through her puffed out cheeks. He stepped politely aside. Liffey smiled again, finally exhaled, and walked slowly over to a waiting cab.

She was on her way!

***

El Diablo and his rider picked their way carefully up the mountain path through the tall pines. It was 3:30 p.m. 'Frank Fitzgerald' could already see the end of the trail. It would not be long now.

***

Mary was making good progress. Her goal was in sight! She could see the huge pile of rocks marking Queen Maeve's grave, like a massive cherry on top of a skyscraper ice cream sundae. Another ten minutes and she would have climbed her first mountain. Maybe. For all she knew, she might have scaled mountains all over the world before amnesia had erased her memory bank.

***

Liffey stopped to catch her breath, and caught a glimpse of the distant figure of a woman who had almost reached the top of Knocknarea. Her heart raced. Somehow she *knew* it was the diamond 'M' lady. A gust of cold wind sent a shiver through her and she was surprised to hear her teeth chattering. The wind brought with it a dense haze and the sky disappeared along with the mottled landscape. It looked like it was going to be another mountain endurance test. "What a surprise," Liffey said cynically, zipping up her jacket and picking up her pace before visibility was completely gone.

CHAPTER THIRTY-SEVEN

Frank Fitzgerald was irritated when he reached the summit and saw clouds sticking to it like clumps of cotton candy. El Diablo, on horse automatic pilot, immediately headed towards the huge mound of rocks which was barely visible through the haze. "This must be part of his regular riding circuit," thought the rider, trying to re-establish mount control. He kicked his heels hard into the surprised horse and harshly reined him to the right. He studied his map and saw that the walking-up trail would be on the other side of the cairn. He would ride over there and wait. He calculated that the cloud cover could actually be a plus for him, because otherwise, there was nowhere to conceal himself and El Diablo on this flat mountain top which was at least half a mile wide. He removed his handgun from its holster under his coat. It was already loaded.

***

Mary could hardly believe she had made it all the way up the mountain. A week ago she could hardly make it out of bed into the kitchen for a cup of coffee and *today* she had climbed a mountain! There was a large boulder just inches from where the path going up ended. She sat down, exhausted, and sipped water from the bottle her driver had insisted she take with her when he discovered she had brought none.

Did she hear a horse whinnying? When she turned around to look, there was nothing but clouds. She hoped Liffey and her father were almost up. "Pretty soon there might be no visibility."

***

When the clouds shifted a bit, Liffey could see there was a woman sitting on what could have been the very rock from which Liffey had watched the videotape with her father. The moment of truth had finally come! In a few minutes, Liffey was hopefully going to find out if the diamond 'M' lady was really Maeve McDermott. A flash of intuition in Chicago had made Liffey think that whoever this lady was, she had to be out of her mind to be living with the loathsome Skunk Man. But if her father was absolutely *certain* that the lady on the tape *was* her mother, she was about to experience something so wonderful it was almost unimaginable, even though she was now only minutes away from it.

Liffey was within shouting distance. She pulled off her blond wig and shook down her real hair. "Hello!" she cried out through cupped hands. The lady stood up from her rock and waved happily. Just as the clouds began to close in again, Liffey could see the lady standing, arms extended, in a welcome home kind of gesture. Liffey felt a tug, as if something was yanking at her and pulling her up the last stretch of the mountain path like she was on an escalator. The clouds shifted once again and blotted out everything. Liffey shouted again, "I'm almost there!"

CHAPTER THIRTY-EIGHT

obert Rivers and his rookie staff investigator, Sam Snyder, went over the plan for the eighth time in the tiny corporate jet as it raced across the Atlantic Ocean towards the northwest coast of Ireland. Louise had stayed behind to coordinate a missing child campaign, using the Rivers Law Office's contacts to set up bulletins throughout the UK and Ireland. A check with Homeland Security revealed that Liffey had purchased a round trip ticket for herself but had also purchased a ticket from Ireland to Chicago for a party named 'Mary Murphy.' Apparently, Liffey planned to return to Chicago on Thursday afternoon with Mary Murphy pending clearance since she had not provided a passport number for Ms. Murphy.

Sam was thrilled to be part of this mission. He was bored interviewing white collar criminals for the Rivers Law Office. He was paid well, but he was young and fit, and eager to take on a mountain search-and-rescue operation. He had climbed the steep rocks at Devil's Lake in Wisconsin many times, and was an experienced hero in his dreams. He was so ready for this.

***

"Liffey? Liffey is that you?" Mary cried out through the pea soup fog. "Be careful you don't slip and…." Her voice suddenly trailed off.

"*Liffey, Run! He's here! Now! Get OUT of here!*" a voice screamed frantically from what had to be the top of the mountain. It was impossible to be sure which direction it was coming from because the fog had now become impenetrable.

"*Mommy? Mommy?*" Liffey screamed hysterically. "*What is it? Who's here? Where are you?*" The silence which followed was deafening, until Liffey heard a horse trotting off in the distance. She was sure it was a horse. Had a horse *kicked* her mother? Knocked her down and then accidentally stomped on her in the in the mist?

She was positive now that the diamond 'M' lady was her mother. She knew it deep down inside, just as surely as she knew how much her father loved her and how much she hated the hornpipe. "I should *never* have called her 'mommy,' Liffey thought despondently. I probably scared her away forever. She obviously has no clue she's my mother, and now I've ruined everything again, just like I did with daddy."

Even though Liffey felt hopeless and alone, she was acutely aware that she *had* to reach her mother and then get them both down the mountain again as quickly as possible. There was no way a horse could follow them down on the narrow hiking path.

There were only a few more yards to go before the summit, when a feeling of dread wrapped itself tightly around Liffey like an ace bandage.

The Skunk Man was up there with her mother! She knew it! Sinead had told her it was possible to ride up one side of the mountain on horseback. He must have ridden a horse up the back mountain trail and surprised her mother. Was it too late? Was her mother dead? Again?

***

Frank Fitzgerald was humming as he dismounted. He reached into a pocket and offered El Diablo a handful of sugar cubes to bribe him to keep quiet. He peered through the shifting clouds at Mary lying inert a few feet away. He had seen the look of terror that streaked across her face when he pistol whipped her head after she screamed out the warning to Liffey Rivers. He was positive the idiot dancer would not retreat, but barge right up the mountain path instead.

He aimed the pistol at Mary's head, but paused. "No. Better to wait. The brat will hear the shot and might run." His horse would not be able to follow her down the steep footpath in the fog. His trap had worked. It was only a matter of minutes until he would be rid of them both forever.

CHAPTER THIRTY-NINE

The Rivers' corporate jet was approaching the northwest coast of Ireland's airspace when Louise called to report that the Sligo Gardai had cancelled a helicopter swat team because of dense fog. They were contacting the Irish army with the hope that there might be another helicopter available in nearby County Donegal which was equipped with infrared equipment to use in adverse conditions. The local Coast Guard in Strandhill did have a helicopter but they were trained rescuers, not gunmen. Robert Rivers could only hope and pray that his daughter would be able to get through this one herself.

In the very back corner of his mind, he also hoped the mystery of the diamond 'M' lady would be solved once and for all. Whoever she was, something told him that she did not intend to harm his daughter. It was her 'brother,' Donald, who needed to be feared. When Robert Rivers had looked into Donald's eyes hiding behind thick glasses at the diamond booth in Chicago, he had seen evil that lenses could not filter.

***

Liffey needed a plan. Her head was throbbing. If she did *not* find a way to get through this, she and her mother might soon be dead. Her mother might be dead already.

The Skunk Man was most likely waiting for her right at the top of this path. She was certain her mother was also there.

She had caught a quick glimpse of her just before the clouds had completely obliterated everything. The warning screams had come at the same time, so her mother had to be directly ahead in the dense fog.

Liffey felt like time was running out, when advice her father had given her many times over the years burst into her head: "*Nothing* is ever as difficult as it seems if you just think *logically.*"

"How can you be *logical* if you are scared to death?"

Liffey could hear her father's reply, "Logic is a greater force than fear, Liffey, because it puts everything into perspective. Use the intelligence heaven gave you and sort out the facts in their order of importance. Then act decisively."

Liffey fell to her knees and scraped the ground with her hands and scooped up a handful of small pebbles. Since *she* could not see, it seemed *logical* that neither could the Skunk Man. She would make him think she was on another path. She could hear the thumping and snorting of an impatient horse nearby. She hurled the pebbles as hard as she could directly to her right. It sounded like a trail hiker who was slipping on the rocks. When she heard the horse slowly moving out, she threw another fistful of pebbles.

When Liffey could no longer hear the careful steps of the tightly controlled horse, she knew it was time to make her move. She stood up and quietly walked forward as quickly as she dared in the thick fog to the top of the trail. When she reached the flat summit, she had no sense of direction. Thinking logically, the Skunk Man and his horse would be disoriented too. This would give Liffey valuable time to search for her mother.

There was only one way to locate someone quickly in this whiteout. In a loud whisper she said, "Anybody out there? It's

Liffey." There was a faint gasping answer somewhere in the middle of the foggy ocean before her. Liffey inched forward towards the voice, and found the diamond 'M' lady, sitting upright on the path with a trickle of blood running down her forehead.

"Liffey? He's *here!* You have *got* to get *out* of here right now. He must have followed me and he intends to murder us. I *saw* the look on his face, Liffey. He has a gun! Go *now* while you can! Forget about me! I don't have the strength to go with you. I will stay here and try to stall him while you get down this mountain. Now please, leave! Please!! This is *all my fault!* I should have never asked you to come here. I do not know *how* I could have done such a thing."

By the time Mary had finished pleading with Liffey to leave, Liffey had helped her to her feet and they began slowly walking along the gravel path together. It was obvious to Liffey that her mother was in no condition to get down the mountain in this fog. She could hardly walk, even with Liffey supporting her. If the fog suddenly lifted, the Skunk Man would be able to shoot at them escaping down the mountain for some distance. They had to hide. "Don't panic," Liffey said comfortingly. "I've been up here before and I'm thinking he probably has *not*. This path leads right to Maeve's cairn. There are tall standing stones we can hide behind when we get closer to the grave. It's a good thing horses can't track us like bloodhounds!"

***

The horseman sat silently. Fuming. He had not heard a sound for five minutes. It must have been a sheep or goat on the mountain which had made the slipping noise. Had Mary's little friend come up the main trail after all?

This thought infuriated him, and he quickly reversed El Diablo, only to realize he had now become completely disoriented. The unrelenting fog had not hinted at letting up, and the rider was not at all confident that he had his bearings anymore. Since he had carelessly forgotten to pack a compass, he had no sense of direction. His only chance, unless the cloud bank lifted, was to give his horse free rein, and hope El Diablo had been programmed by the riding stables to go to the cairn and trot around it. If he got to the cairn, he could regroup.

Fog or no fog, he was not leaving this mountain until he had finished what he had come up here to do.

CHAPTER FORTY

L iffey dialed Sinead's mobile and carefully placed the light blanket she had thought to bring along with her across her mother's trembling shoulders as they huddled together under a tall standing stone in the thick fog. Liffey was worried that her mother was having a convulsion, because her eyes were glassy and she was not able to talk any longer. "Sinead! Thank God you answered," Liffey said hoarsely. "I need your help. I'm in big trouble."

***

Robert Rivers was relieved that they were given clearance to land at Knock International Airport. Apparently fog was not a problem in County Mayo this evening at 6:00 p.m. He had heard nothing about Liffey from the Gardai, and it had been two hours now since Liffey was to have met the diamond 'M' lady on the summit of Knocknarea. He had never known such fear. Liffey had tried to call him once about an hour ago but she had been cut off. He began to prepare himself for the worst possible explanation. She had not called back because she was not *able* to call back.

Sam Snyder studied the map of Knocknarea Louise had given him. If the helicopter could not land on the summit, he would be lowered down and continue on foot. Robert Rivers would do the same but Sam knew his employer was exhausted and weak. "It's all up to me," he thought, checking his field equipment one last time.

***

Maeve was slumped down now, propped against an ancient, weathered stone, sleeping. Liffey waited breathlessly for the inevitable attack. She had assembled a pile of stones to throw to draw the horse rider away from her comatose mother. She was *not* going to abandon her. She had not heard back from Sinead yet and hoped her friend had not completely freaked out and locked herself in a closet or something. "I'll bet Sinead wishes she had never told me after the Beltra Feis that it would be fun to do this kind of thing every day," Liffey thought tensely.

***

The clip-clop of approaching horse hooves penetrated the stillness like spikes being hammered into hard ground. They sounded far away, but it was impossible to tell *how* far in the merciless fog. Liffey planted a kiss on Maeve's forehead, and gently told her she would not let anything happen to her.

Liffey was quivering with fear as she slowly stood up to face her assailant. Maeve did not open her eyes. Liffey took her plastic rain gear from her backpack and spread it over her mother to insulate her from a cold wind which had begun to drastically lower the temperature. She took off her jacket and gently placed it behind Maeve's head and the standing stone.

Liffey's phone vibrated inside her jean pocket. It was Sinead! "Liffey, I'm more than half way up the mountain. I've got *both* my older brothers with me. We'll be there soon." Liffey was horrified. "Sinead, you *can't* come up here with your *brothers!* I thought you would send the Gardai!"

"Liffey, my brothers *are* the Gardai. They're undercover drug enforcement officers in Dublin. They just happened to be home visiting with us today. They're used to chasing people all over the place and being shot at." Liffey marveled at Sinead's ability to get things done and whispered, "Thanks Sinead. Gotta go now. He's coming. I hear his horse. We're at the first standing stone next to the cairn on your left. I have to draw him away from my mother." "Your *what?*" Sinead demanded. "I thought you told me your mum was *dead*, Liffey?" "Not anymore, Sinead, and I want to keep it that way. Thanks for all your help. Please send your brothers to my mother. She's unconscious and I think she's in bad shape. I'll check in when I get to another hiding place. Could you have them blow a whistle or something when they get to her? Just so I know she'll make it? "

***

The helicopter left Knock Airport, and headed towards County Sligo and Knocknarea. The pilot had good news. "The fog is supposed to be lifting a bit now, Mr. Rivers. So I might very well be able to put her down. I've done rescues on that mountain before and it can be tricky. But I am trickier," he said with a big grin.

***

The clip-clopping hooves were very close now. This was not a bad dream and there was not going to be a 'Chicken Dance' alarm wake-up reprieve. "This is really it," Liffey realized with a sickening feeling. "I am right down to it in a real life or death situation. I have to do something right *now* to draw him away from my mother."

151

Liffey threw a small rock in the direction of the horse to create a diversion. Then she selected her 'Chicken Dance' ring tones on her cell phone and threw it as hard as she could towards the huge cairn which had now become intermittently visible through the rolling clouds. The huge mound of rocks looked to be about thirty feet from her. She could faintly hear the obnoxious mobile ring tones in the distance. Was she imagining it, or was the horse stepping towards the song?

She took this opportunity to move left and away from her mother. The ring tones grew fainter. She had to make sure that the Skunk Man did not get anywhere near the standing stones or her mother would be his first victim. He had already harmed her with a savage blow to her head. There was nothing else to do but shout out to him to draw him away. She could *not* just keep throwing rocks. She was determined her mother was not going to be the second Maeve lying dead up here. She would keep him moving and if she made him angry enough, he might forget about her mother and keep after her alone in the fog.

"Hey, Mr. McFleury! Are you judging a feis up here today? Come and judge my hornpipe if you can find me!"

Liffey did not quite believe she had said that, but it was too late now. She might as well jump head first into this. She heard the horse advancing in her direction, away from the standing stones. It had worked! Liffey bolted straight ahead and called out again mockingly, *"Smuggling any diamonds today?"*

The stress of running and shouting taunting 'come and get me' remarks was beginning to take its toll, but Liffey knew she had to keep dodging until Sinead's brothers arrived and managed to get her mother to safety. Was it her imagination, or were the clouds beginning to lift, like they finally did a few days ago when she and her father had been stuck up here? If they *were* breaking up, she would need to take cover fast and as far away from her mother's standing stone as she could possibly get. She knew she would not be able to outrun a horse. She would just have to keep moving as long as she could until help arrived.

***

El Diablo was moving steadily away from Maeve's cairn towards the mocking voice coming out of the fog. The rider removed the safety from his handgun and looked through the clouds for his target. The next time he heard her voice, he would shoot blindly at it.

***

Liffey had been running for a long time. She was tired and running out of breath. She had probably covered half a mile or more, barely keeping out of the horseman's limited range of vision in the fog when she heard the horse whinny not a hundred feet from her, and a voice triumphantly bellow, "I've found you!"

The horse thundered towards her. Liffey turned and ran. The horse came closer and closer. She turned away from its great black shadow moving straight at her through the fog. In a second, she would be visible. In desperation, she threw herself behind a small gorse bush, and flattened her body against it, wincing with pain as the thorns pierced her flesh. The horseman passed her by.

Liffey bit her lip hard to avoid screaming out in pain caused by hundreds of spiky thorns piercing her back and arms. Just at the point when she was unable to keep her sobs muffled for one more second, she heard the roar of several helicopters approaching the mountain. The fog was definitely lifting now.

This was good and bad. Good, because maybe the helicopters were looking for her, and bad because it might already be too late. Still, the rider had not yet found her, and the obvious horse sounds were no longer nearby. She stood up painfully and saw she was near what appeared to be the edge of a cliff. Perhaps there was a ledge she could get down to, unseen.

But he was close! She could feel a malevolent presence waiting to pierce her just like the thorns on the gorse bush.

She turned and saw the shiny black horse coming at her once again through the mist. Something in her terrified brain remembered that if a tornado is coming directly at you, you are supposed to run at right angles away from it. Liffey was thinking about this now, and about how would you ever be able to *know* if you were actually running in a right angle away from a tornado, when she heard a whistle blowing in the distance, far away. It was followed by a loud crack. Liffey smiled with relief as she felt the ground going out from underneath her feet.

CHAPTER FORTY-ONE

Robert Rivers watched the helicopter leaving the mountain, carrying the two people he loved most in the world.

He had recognized Maeve the instant he laid eyes upon her wrapped up in Liffey's rain gear. She had hardly changed in ten long years. Maeve remained unconscious and had not opened her eyes since the McGowan brothers had carried her from the standing stones to the helicopter.

Liffey smiled weakly at her father through the glass helicopter door. She had slipped and hit her forehead on a large rock at the edge of a cliff. Her arms were swollen to twice their size from hundreds of gorse thorn punctures. Her back felt like someone had given her fifty lashes. "I'll meet both of you at the hospital, Liffey," Robert Rivers shouted over the whapping helicopter din.

***

Sam Snyder told the Gardai that just as he was being lowered by the helicopter, he had seen a large black horse stop cold at the edge of a cliff, ejecting its rider over the precipice like a sling-shot. Then the stallion turned abruptly, and calmly trotted off into the mist like Black Beauty.

In the gathering darkness, the Gardai had left the scene to look for the thrown rider on the west side of Knocknarea.

Sam told Robert Rivers that, after he touched ground, he ran over to Liffey who was lying face down next to the precipice.

While the medics from the Army helicopter were working on her, he walked over to the cliff and looked down. There was no sign of the rider, but it was hard to make out anything clearly through the mist. He managed to climb down a few feet on to a narrow ledge. From there, he determined it would be a death fall so he turned back.

Sam could tell that his employer was finally mentally spent. He did not think Robert Rivers had slept a minute on their transatlantic flight. He would tell him some other time about the strange bones he had seen when he was climbing back up from the ledge.

***

As Sam carefully edged his way back up, he was startled to see a pronounced fissure in the mountain rock which was barely wide enough for him to peer into. He aimed the small light on his safety helmet through the slit and saw a large pile of bones in the center of a small cave. He could not make out if they were animal or human. There was also what appeared to be a human skeleton propped up against the far wall. It seemed to have some kind of metal armor draped over it and was holding a lance or spear in its skeletal fist. "Things over here in Ireland are certainly dramatic," he thought. "I'll try to remember to tell Attorney Rivers about this when he gets back to the office."

***

Liffey's father sat down on the same boulder where he and Liffey had watched the voice from the grave video a little over four days ago. Everything seemed murky and dreamlike. Sinead came over to him and gently took his hand. Her sturdy brothers hoisted Robert Rivers back up on to his feet. "Come on now," she said. "We need to be getting you down this mountain and to hospital so you can be with Liffey and her mum. I know you're after having a long day, but you have a family to look after, Mr. Rivers."

CHAPTER FORTY-TWO

Even though Liffey had not practiced any Irish dance steps since she found her mother, and she was still very sore from her injuries, she very much wanted to compete at the Fall Festival Feis in Milwaukee and her Aunt Jean said she could. This green light from Aunt Jean had not really surprised Liffey. She knew her father would have *never* given her permission to dance so soon after a serious head injury. Aunt Jean, on the other hand, pretty much acted like she herself had a serious head injury most of the time.

Aunt Jean was totally vacant. You could eat pizza for breakfast, lunch and dinner with Aunt Jean. Or not eat at all. You could stay up and read all night without sneaking with a flashlight. Or sit up in the den and watch the all night movie channel.

Ever since Aunt Jean had met Liffey at the Dublin Airport to accompany her back to Wisconsin, Liffey had been able to get *whatever* she wanted, *whenever* she wanted it. Aunt Jean obviously felt sorry for Liffey and Liffey took full advantage of her aunt's pity. Liffey *hated* to risk going to another feis with her aunt but could not think of any alternatives. Her father would be staying in Ireland until her mother woke up and that could be weeks yet. Aunt Jean was in charge of her until then and she seemed absolutely *thrilled* about going to the feis. This enthusiasm worried Liffey somewhat but she had no other choice.

Friday night, Liffey and her aunt prepared the ritualistic pre-feis spaghetti and meatballs dinner. Liffey could hardly believe she had to *show* her aunt how to make meatballs! Aunt Jean had obviously grown up on Mars. Tomorrow, Liffey would assemble her own pre-feis breakfast with a bagel, slice of turkey, cheese and tomato. She would make sure she stayed totally clear of Aunt Jean after breakfast. Aunt Jean might very well be planning an early morning pep-rally to get Liffey in a competitive mood.

***

Liffey's cell phone was somewhere up on Knocknarea, and she only woke up now because Max the Magnificent was whining to be let out. Aunt Jean was apparently already up. Liffey could hear her aunt moving around in the guest room. "Why did she forget to wake me up?" Liffey griped, already irritated with her aunt's irresponsible behavior.

Liffey had packed her solo dress and other dance supplies before she went to bed last night, but she was still angry that her aunt had evidently forgotten all about her.

The mystery of Aunt Jean's forgetfulness was cleared up quickly. Just before Liffey reached the kitchen, the door to the guest room flew open and Aunt Jean stepped perkily out into the hallway in a dark green, *adult Irish dancer dress!* To Liffey's horror, she was even wearing a wig. Most adult dancers did *not* wear wigs. Aunt Jean looked like Marie Antoinette, with platinum blond curls piled high on her head. She was even wearing a diamond tiara. A tiara? How old *was* Aunt Jean anyway? Twelve?

"Liffey, darling! *This* is the surprise I told your father about! Can you please watch *me* dance today? It will be my very *first feis* and I'm terribly nervous!"

Liffey was speechless. Apparently, she was supposed to be concerned now about how her *totally* old Aunt Jean would dance today. "Like I don't already have enough *me* to worry about!"

Trying to put a positive spin on her aunt's horrific revelation was going to be hard, but a glimmer of hope quickly switched on in Liffey's overtaxed head. "If Aunt Jean *is* dancing today, then she might not *follow me around* to my stages and embarrass me to death. *And*, Aunt Jean will probably want to go everywhere on earth for competitions and bring me *with* her!"

"That's just *great*!" Liffey said enthusiastically. "It's really *great* you became an Irish dancer, Aunt Jean!"

Aunt Jean smiled modestly and adjusted her tiara in the hall mirror.

CHAPTER FORTY-THREE

As Maeve McDermott's eyes fluttered open in Ireland on Saturday afternoon, and Liffey Rivers and her Aunt Jean were driving northeast in Wisconsin early Saturday morning, a September Blood Moon was already rising in South Africa.

The pale little boy watched the reddish-gold orb coming up from behind the jagged hills as he wheeled his chair into the river of moonlight flowing through the skylight of the reception room at the Holy Infant Home for Disabled Children.

No one was ever in there, but he went anyway. If he did not check, he might miss his parents if they ever came looking for him.

THE END

A BROCKAGH BOOK

www.liffeyrivers.com

LIFFEY'S LINGO

Aer Lingus: (Air-LING-us) This is the airline I take when I go to Ireland. It comes from the word 'aerloingeas' which means air fleet in Irish.

Ballysadare: (Bal'-lee-sa-DARE) A part of Sligo Bay next to Knocknarea, and a small town between Sligo Town and Beltra.

Beltra: (bell-TRAH) This word means 'mouth of the strand.' But there is no beach there. At least, not at the 'beltra' where I was in County Sligo when I danced at the Beltra Feis.

Cairn: A really big pile of rocks. People were buried under them thousands of years ago. Queen Maeve's cairn is one of the biggest ones. You can see cairns on top of lots of mountains in County Sligo.

Connaught: (KON-nut) The western part of Ireland where Sligo is.

Feis: (Fesh) This word means a kind of festival or get together. But to Irish dancers, it means a dance competition.

Feiseanna: (fesh-ON-ah) I am positive this means more than one feis. Plural.

Gardai: (gar-DEE) This is what you call policemen in Irish. One policeman is a garda. More than one garda are called the gardai.

Knocknarea: (nock'-na-RAY) This is the mountain where everything seems to happen to me. It is in County Sligo, Ireland, with Maeve's cairn or tomb on the top.

Liffey: (LIF-ee) Just in case you never heard my name pronounced out loud and thought I was named after that other river in Ireland, this is my name. It is also the river that runs straight through Dublin with all the famous bridges. It is really called the 'Anna Liffey' but people just say 'the Liffey.'

Maeve: (MAYV) Queen Maeve lived about 2,000 years ago. She was queen of Connaught and a fierce warrior.

Sinead: (Shin-AID) Sinead is a very popular girls' name in Ireland. It means 'gracious' and I believe it because my friend Sinead is the nicest person I have ever met.

Sligo: (SLY-go) I am pretty sure this word means 'place of the shells.' In Irish, it is called Sligeach: (SHLEE-gock) It is the name of a county in Connaught, and also a big city.

Made in the
USA
Monee, IL